# SAFE ENOUGH
## AND OTHER STORIES

# SAFE ENOUGH

## AND OTHER STORIES

## LEE CHILD

THE MYSTERIOUS PRESS
NEW YORK

SAFE ENOUGH AND OTHER STORIES

Mysterious Press
An Imprint of Penzler Publishers
58 Warren Street
New York, NY 10007

"Addicted to Sweetness," first published in *MWA Presents the Rich and the Dead*, edited by Nelson DeMille (© 2011).
"The Bodyguard," first published in *First Thrills*, edited by Lee Child (© 2010).
"The Bone-Headed League," first published in *A Study in Sherlock*, edited by Laurie R. King and Leslie S. Klinger (© 2011).
"Dying for a Cigarette," first published in *The Nicotine Chronicles*, edited by Lee Child (© 2020).
"The .50 Solution," first published in *Bloodlines: A Horse Racing Anthology*, edited by Maggie Estep and Jason Starr (© 2006).
"The Greatest Trick of All," first published in *Greatest Hits*, edited by Robert J. Randisi (© 2007).
"I Heard a Romantic Story," first published in *Love Is Murder*, edited by Sandra Brown (© 2012).
"Me & Mr. Rafferty," first published in *The Dark End of the Street*, edited by Jonathan Santlofer and S. J. Rozan (© 2010).
"My First Drug Trial," first published in *The Marijuana Chronicles*, edited by Jonathan Santlofer (© 2013).
"New Blank Document," first published in *It Occurs to Me That I Am America*, edited by Jonathan Santlofer (© 2018).
"Normal in Every Way," first published in *Deadly Anniversaries*, edited by Marcia Muller and Bill Pronzini (© 2020).
"Pierre, Lucien, and Me," first published in *Alive in Shape and Color*, edited by Lawrence Block (© 2017).
"Public Transportation," first published in *Phoenix Noir*, edited by Patrick Millikin (© 2009).
"Safe Enough," first published in *MWA Presents Death Do Us Part*, edited by Harlan Coben (© 2006).
"Section 7 (a) (Operational)," first published in *Agents of Treachery*, edited by Otto Penzler (© 2010).
"Shorty and the Briefcase," first published in *Ten Year Stretch*, edited by Martin Edwards and Adrian Muller (© 2018).
"The Snake Eater by the Numbers," first published in *Like a Charm*, edited by Karin Slaughter (© 2004).
"Ten Keys," first published in *The Cocaine Chronicles*, edited by Jervey Tervalon and Gary Phillips (© 2005).
"The Truth About What Happened," first published in *In Sunlight or in Shadow: Stories Inspired by the Paintings of Edward Hopper*, edited by Lawrence Block (© 2016).
"Wet with Rain," first published in *Belfast Noir*, edited by Adrian McKinty and Stuart Neville (© 2014).

First edition

Interior design by Maria Fernandez

Library of Congress Control Number: 2024940193

Hardcover ISBN: 978-1-61316-566-9
eBook ISBN: 978-1-61316-571-3

10  9  8  7  6  5  4  3  2  1

Printed in the United States of America
Distributed by W. W. Norton & Company

*For my longtime friend Otto Penzler, whose idea this was.*

# CONTENTS

# FOREWORD

In the early 1990s I was fifteen years into a career in TV production, but the winds of change were blowing, and I sensed the gravy train couldn't run forever. So what next? I hatched a vague, simmering plan to write novels, but mostly forgot about it, because day to day and month to month I was still very busy. Then eventually, like Hemingway had said of bankruptcy, the end that had been at first approaching gradually became suddenly sudden. One day I was a veteran director; the next day I was unemployed.

It was time to put the standby plan into action.

I had taught myself to read at the age of three and graduated to books without pictures at the age of four, and since then had read probably ten thousand long-form narrative works. I had forty thousand hours of television under my belt, both drama and documentary. I felt I had a decent working knowledge of popular entertainment, its rhythms and grammars, of what big audiences want, of why they react as they do, and why some things work for them, and some don't. I was familiar with what we call the agented professions. I figured that the acquiring editors at publishing houses would be similar to the commissioning producers in TV. I understood promotion and publicity. Reading was always my first and best love and I felt the mix of personal passion combined with wider entertainment experience would help me. I knew from hard lessons that precisely nothing in showbiz is guaranteed but, overall, I felt I had a reasonable chance of making it as a novelist. As good as anyone else, probably, and maybe better than some. I was prepared. I had looked ahead and thought hard. I felt I had it mostly figured out. I was ready to go.

I had overlooked short stories completely.

I knew what they were, obviously. I had read and enjoyed hundreds. The best of them struck me as small, intricate, perfectly formed items, like Fabergé eggs. A couple have lived on in my memory for decades and no doubt will forever. But I had never thought of writing them. Instinctively I didn't see the connection between long form and short form. I thought there wasn't one. I thought they were handled by totally different people. I wasn't aware that a genre author like me would be asked to try both.

I finished my first novel and fed it into the machine, where happily it was accepted and slated for publication about eighteen months in the future. I knew that if I wanted to publish a book a year, then I would have to write a book a year, so I spent that eighteen-month delay writing my second novel and most of the third. (I was following advice from an old sports coach, who told me: You can't grow more talent, but you can make damn sure you work harder than the other guy.) All three books came in well over a hundred thousand words each, full of, I hoped, exciting and propulsive action and suspense, but also light and shade, with quiet scenes and minor diversions—all the things that make novels such spacious and accommodating canvases, delightful first to the author, and later (again, I hoped) to the reader.

My first novel came out in the spring of 1997. Jack Reacher was introduced to the world. He was greeted as a relative success and the book was seen as the debut installment in what might possibly become a successful series. Those verdicts prompted two immediate results—first, a movie option from Hollywood and, second, a request for a short story. I was somewhat familiar with Hollywood—my old TV company had opened a movie arm and won two Oscars first time out—but I needed a crash course in the short story ecosystem.

I was introduced to the world of anthologies. Some were straightforward attempts by publishers to make a minor profit; some were retrospective "best of" celebrations of recent writing, gathered from here and there and curated by specialists; some were charity ventures aiming to use donated content to raise money for worthy causes. But most were fundraisers put together by writers' organizations—Mystery Writers of America, International Thriller Writers, and so on—who would pay their bills out of the royalty income such volumes would generate (they hoped).

Naturally that income would be greater if those volumes were filled by already-established superstars, but writers' organizations are there to help us all, so the norm seemed to be a fifty-fifty split between big names and new names. Devoted readers would buy the anthologies because of the big names and the new names would benefit (we hoped) from the association and exposure. The final piece of information I gleaned was that for all these reasons, whoever you were, writing short stories was basically pro bono. No individual writer ever made significant money from them. This was borne out by my own subsequent experience, in which my best-performing short story has made thousands of times less than my worst-performing novel. In the long run, for me at least, that disparity turned out to be the best thing about short stories.

So, thus informed, with two-and-a-bit novels written and one so far published, I supplied a short story to a crime fiction anthology. Then someone else asked, and then another someone else, and so on, until I was writing five or six a year. Or ten. Sometimes more, probably. Each time I had to make a basic binary decision—whether to write a Reacher story or a non-Reacher.

I mixed it up from the beginning. Using Reacher had advantages—a pre-supplied character and structure, an established voice and grammar, a chance to use ideas or plot fragments not durable enough for a novel, and so on.

But the non-Reacher stories were the real delight for me. The volume you're reading now is the editor's pick of them. For me the joy was stepping out and trying something different every time. Something new. Period, place, nationality, personality, every-thing. It was liberating. And fun. What made it even better was a conviction my deep-down subconscious was getting totally wrong. As mentioned, none of these stories made any money. Therefore, my box office–trained subconscious said, no one was reading them. No audience, no money. That's show business.

The illusion that no one was watching was the best thing ever. It made the stakes nonexistent. I tried anything I wanted. Some were failures, but others really caught the voice I had in my head. I was happy with them. Although I'm not sure I ever really learned to write them. Not well. Fabergé eggs they ain't. There's a mysterious short story thing the great writers do. I never figured it out. Mine are very, very, very short novels. But none the worse for it. They have beginnings and middles and ends. Something surprising happens. Or is revealed.

What they show me now is not only the undeniable flow and energy created by pastures new and no one watching, but also—in retrospect—created by the absence of a subliminal sense on the writer's part that there's much, much more to come. That there is a boulder to be rolled up the hill. There's no caution about parceling stuff out. No need to save anything for Chapter 17. It's all right there, right now, racing through with abandon, often written in one take at one sitting. Like I said, it was fun.

—Lee Child
Colorado
2024

# THE BODYGUARD

Like everything else, the world of bodyguarding is split between the real and the phony. Phony bodyguards are just glorified drivers, big men in suits chosen for their size and shape and appearance, not paid very much, not very useful when push comes to shove. Real bodyguards are technicians, thinkers, trained men with experience. They can be small, as long as they can think and endure. As long as they can be useful, when the time comes.

I am a real bodyguard.

Or at least, I was.

I was trained in one of those secret army regiments where close personal protection is part of the curriculum. I plied that trade among many others for a long time, all over the world. I am a medium-sized man, lean, fast, full of stamina. Not quite a marathon runner, but nothing like a weightlifter. I left the army after fifteen years of service and took jobs through an agency run by a friend. Most of the work was in South and Central America. Most of the engagements were short.

I got into it right when the business was going crazy.

Kidnapping for ransom was becoming a national sport in most of the South American nations. If you were rich or politically connected, you were automatically a target. I worked for British and American corporate clients. They had managers and executives in places like Panama and Brazil and Colombia. Those people were considered infinitely rich and infinitely connected. Rich, because their employers were likely to bail them out, and those corporations were capitalized in the hundreds of billions. Connected, because ultimately the Western governments would get involved. There was no greater sense of connection than a bad guy knowing he could sit in a jungle clearing somewhere and be heard in 10 Downing Street or the White House.

But I never lost a client. I was a good technician, and I had good clients. All of them knew the stakes. They worked with me. They were biddable and obedient. They wanted to do their two years in the heat and get back alive to their head offices and their promotions. They kept their heads down, didn't go out at night, didn't really go anywhere except their offices and their job sites. All transport was at high speed in protected vehicles, by varied routes, and at unpredictable times. My clients never complained. Because they were working, they tended to accept a rough equivalent of military discipline. It was all relatively easy, for a while.

Then I went private.

The money was better. The work was worse. I learned to stay away from people who wanted a bodyguard purely as a status symbol. There were plenty of those. They made me miserable, because ultimately there wasn't much for me to do. Too many times I ended up running errands while my skills eroded. I learned to stay away from people who weren't in genuine need, too. London is a dangerous town and New York is worse, but nobody truly needs a bodyguard in either place. Again, not much to do. Boring, and corrosive. I freely admit that my own risk addiction drove my decisions.

Including my decision to work for Anna.

I'm still not allowed to mention her second name. It was in my contract, and my contract binds me until I die. I heard about the opening through a friend of a friend. I was flown to Paris for the interview. Anna turned out to be twenty-two years old, unbelievably pretty, dark, slender, mysterious. First surprise, she conducted the interview herself. Mostly in a situation like that the father handles things. Like hiring a bodyguard is the same kind of undertaking as buying a Mercedes convertible for a birthday present. Or arranging riding lessons.

But Anna was different.

She was rich in her own right. She had an inheritance from a separate branch of the family. I think she was actually richer than her old man, who was plenty rich to start with. The mother was rich, too. Separate money again. They were Brazilian. The father was a businessman and a politician. The mother was a local TV star. It was a triple whammy. Oceans of cash, connections, Brazil.

I should have walked away.

But I didn't. I suppose I wanted the challenge. And Anna was captivating. Not that a close personal relationship would have been appropriate. She was a client and I was close to twice her age. But from the first moments I knew she would be fun to be around. The interview went well. She took my formal qualifications for granted. I have scars and medals and commendations. I had never lost a client. Anything else, she wouldn't have been talking to me, of course. She asked about my world view, my opinions, my tastes, my preferences. She was interested in compatibility issues. Clearly she had employed bodyguards before.

She asked how much freedom I would give her.

She said she did charity work in Brazil. Human rights, poverty relief, the usual kind of thing. Hours and days of travel in the slums and the outlying jungle. I told her about my previous South American clients. The corporate guys, the oilmen, the minerals people. I told her that the less they did, the safer they got. I described their normal day. Home, car, office, car, home.

She said no to that.

She said, "We need to find a balance."

Her native language was Portuguese, and her English was good but lightly accented. She sounded even better than she looked, which was spectacular. She wasn't one of those rich girls who dress down. No ripped jeans for her. For the interview she was wearing a pair of plain black pants and a white shirt. Both garments looked new, and I was sure both came from an exclusive Paris boutique.

I said, "Pick a number. I can keep you a hundred percent safe by keeping you here in your apartment twenty-four seven, or you can be a hundred percent unsafe by walking around Rio on your own all day."

"Seventy-five percent safe," she said. Then she shook her head. "No, eighty."

I knew what she was saying. She was scared, but she wanted a life. She was unrealistic.

I said, "Eighty percent means you live Monday through Thursday and die on Friday."

She went quiet.

"You're a prime target," I said. "You're rich, your mom is rich, your dad is rich, and he's a politician. You'll be the best target in Brazil. And kidnapping is a messy business. It usually fails. It's usually the same thing as murder, just delayed by a little. Sometimes delayed by not very much."

She said nothing.

"And it's sometimes very unpleasant," I said. "Panic, stress, desperation. You wouldn't be kept in a gilded cage. You'd be in a jungle hut with a bunch of thugs."

"I don't want a gilded cage," she said. "And you'll be there."

I knew what she was saying. She was twenty-two years old.

"We'll do our best," I said.

She hired me there and then. Paid me an advance on a very generous salary and asked me to make a list of what I needed. Guns, clothes, cars. I didn't ask for anything. I thought I had what I needed.

I thought I knew what I was doing.

———

A week later we were in Brazil. We flew first class all the way, Paris to London, London to Miami, Miami to Rio. My choice of route. Indirect and unpredictable. Thirteen hours in the air, five in airport lounges. She was a pleasant companion, and a cooperative client. I had a friend pick us up in Rio. Anna had budget to spare, so I decided to use a separate driver at all times. That way, I would get more chance to concentrate. I used a Russian guy I had met in Mexico. He was the finest defensive driver I had ever seen. Russians are great with cars. They have to be. Moscow was the only place worse than Rio for mayhem.

Anna had her own apartment. I had been expecting a gated place in the suburbs, but she lived right in town. A good thing, in a way. One street entrance, a doorman, a concierge, plenty of eyes on visitors even before the elevator bank. The apartment door was steel and it had three locks and a TV entryphone. I like TV entryphones a lot better than peepholes. Peepholes are very bad ideas. A guy can wait in the corridor and as soon as the lens goes dark he can fire a large caliber handgun right through it, into your eye, into your brain, out the back of your skull, into your client if she happens to be standing behind you.

So, a good situation. My Russian friend parked in the garage under the building and we took the elevator straight up and got inside and locked all three locks and settled in. I had a room between Anna's and the door. I'm a light sleeper. All was well.

All stayed well for less than twenty-four hours.

Jet lag going west wakes you up early. We were both up at seven. Anna wanted breakfast out. Then she planned to go shopping. I hesitated. The first decision sets the tone. But I was her bodyguard, not her jailer. So I agreed. Breakfast, and shopping.

Breakfast was OK. We went to a hotel, for a long slow meal in the dining room. The place was full of bodyguards. Some were real, some were phony. Some were at separate tables, some were eating with their clients. I ate with Anna. Fruit, coffee, croissants. She ate more than I did. She was full of energy and raring to go.

It all went wrong with the shopping.

Later I realized my Russian friend had sold me out. Because usually the first day is the easiest. Who even knows you're in town? But my guy must have made a well-timed phone call. Anna and I came out of a store and our car wasn't on the curb. Anna was carrying her own packages. I had made clear that she would from the start. I'm a bodyguard, not a porter, and I need my hands free. I glanced left and saw nothing. I glanced right and saw four guys with guns.

The guys were close to us and the guns were small automatics, black, new, still dewy with oil. The guys were small, fast, wiry. The street was busy. Crowds behind me, crowds behind the four guys. Traffic on my left, the store doorway on my right. Certain collateral damage if I pulled out my own gun and started firing. Protracted handgun engagements always produce a lot of stray bullets. Innocent casualties would have been high.

And I would have lost, anyway.

Winning four-on-one gun battles is strictly for the movies. My job was to keep Anna alive, even if it was just for another day. Or another hour. The guys moved in and took my gun and stripped Anna of her packages and pinned her arms. A white car pulled up on cue and we were forced inside. Anna first, then me. We were sandwiched on the back seat between two guys who shoved guns in our ribs. Another guy in the front seat twisted around and pointed another gun at us. The driver took off fast. Within a minute we were deep into a tangle of side streets.

I had been wrong about the jungle hut. We were taken to an abandoned office building inside the city limits. It was built of brick and painted a dusty white. I had been right about the thugs. The building teemed with them. There was a whole gang. At least forty of them. They were dirty and uncouth and most of them were leering openly at Anna. I hoped they weren't going to separate us.

They separated us immediately. I was thrown in a cell that had once been an office. There was a heavy iron grille over the window and a big lock on the door. A bed, and a bucket. That was all. The bed was a hospital cot made of metal tubes. The bucket was empty, but it hadn't been empty for long. It smelled. I was put in handcuffs with my arms pinned behind my back. My ankles were shackled and I was dumped on the floor. I was left alone for three hours.

Then the nightmare started.

The lock rattled and the door opened and a guy came in. He looked like the boss. Tall, dark, a wide unsmiling mouth full of gold teeth. He kicked me twice in the ribs and explained that this was a political kidnapping. Some financial gain was expected as a bonus, but the real aim was to use Anna as leverage against her politician father to get a government inquiry stopped. She was the ace up their sleeve. I was expendable. I would be killed within a few hours. Nothing personal, the guy said. Then he said I would be killed in a way that his men would find entertaining. They were bored, and he owed them a diversion. He was planning to let them decide the exact manner of my demise.

Then I was left alone again.

———

Much later I learned that Anna was locked in a similar room two floors away. She was not in handcuffs or ankle shackles. She was free to move around, as befitted her elevated status. Her furniture was basically the same as mine. An iron hospital bed, but no bucket. She had a proper bathroom. And a table, and a chair. She was going to be fed. She was valuable to them.

And she was brave.

As soon as the door locked she started looking for a weapon. The chair was a possibility. Or she could smash the bathroom sink and use a jagged shard of porcelain as a knife. But she wanted something better. She looked at the bed. It was bolted together from iron tubes, flattened and flanged at the ends. The mattress was a thin thing covered with striped ticking. She hauled it off and dumped it on the floor. The bed had a base of metal mesh suspended between two long tubes. The long tubes had a single bolt through each end.

If she could get one free she would have a spear six feet, six inches long. But the bed frame was painted and the bolts were jammed solid. She tried to turn them with her fingers, but it was hopeless. The room was hot and she had a sheen of sweat on her skin and her fingers just slipped. She put the mattress back and turned her attention to the table.

The table had four legs and a veneered top about three feet square. Surrounding it was a short bracing skirt. Upside down it would have looked like a very shallow box. The legs were bolted onto small angled metal braces that were fixed to the skirt. The bolts were cheap steel, a little brassy in color. The nuts were wingnuts. They could be turned easily by hand. She unfastened one leg and hid the nut and the bolt. Left the leg where it was, propped up and vertical.

Then she sat on the bed and waited.

After an hour she heard footsteps in the corridor. Heard the lock turn. A man stepped into the room, carrying a tray of food. He was young. Presumably low man on the totem pole, confined to kitchen duties. He had a gun on his hip. A black automatic pistol, big and boxy and brand new.

Anna stood up and said, "Put the tray on the bed. I think there's something wrong with the table."

The young man lowered the tray onto the mattress. Anna asked, "Where's my friend?"

"What friend?"

"My bodyguard."

"In his room," the guy said. "But not for long. Pretty soon he'll be downstairs and we'll be having some fun with him."

"What kind of fun?"

"I'm not sure. But I'm sure it'll be something pretty imaginative."

"A game?"

"Not exactly. We're going to kill him."

"Why?"

"Because we don't need him."

Anna said nothing.

The boy said, "What's wrong with the table?"

"One of the legs is loose."

"Which one?"

"This one," Anna said, and whipped the leg out. She swung it like a baseball bat and caught the guy square in the face with it. The edge of the corner hit him on the bridge of the nose and punched a shard of bone backward into his brain pan. He was dead before he hit the floor. Anna took the gun off his hip and stepped over his body and walked to the door.

The gun said *Glock* on the side. There was no safety mechanism on it. Anna hooked her finger around the trigger and stepped out to the corridor. *Downstairs*, the boy had said. She found a staircase and went down and kept on going.

———

By that point they had dragged me to a large ground floor room. A conference hall, maybe, once upon a time. There were thirty-nine people in it. There was a small raised stage with two chairs on it. The boss man was in one of them. They put me in the other. Then they all started discussing something in Portuguese. How to kill me, I presumed. How to maximize their entertainment. Halfway through a door opened in the back of the room. Anna stepped in, swinging a large handgun from side to side in front of her. Reaction was immediate. Thirty-eight men pulled out weapons of their own and pointed them at her.

But the boss man didn't. Instead he yelled an urgent warning. I didn't speak his language, but I knew what he was saying. He was saying, *Don't shoot her! We need her alive! She's valuable to us!* The thirty-eight guys lowered their guns and watched as Anna moved through them. She reached the stage. The boss man smiled.

"You've got seventeen shells in that gun," he said. "There are thirty-nine of us here. You can't shoot us all."

Anna nodded.

"I know," she said. Then she turned the gun on herself and pressed it into her chest. "But I can shoot myself."

After that, it was easy. She made them unlock my cuffs and my chains. I took a gun from the nearest guy and we backed out of the room. And we got away with it. Not by threatening to shoot our pursuers, but by Anna threatening to shoot herself, with me backing her up. Five minutes later we were in a taxi. Thirty minutes later we were home.

A day later I quit the bodyguarding business. Because I took it as a sign. A guy who needs to be rescued by his client has no future, except as a phony.

# THE GREATEST TRICK OF ALL

I could have shot you in one ear and out the other from a thousand yards. I could have brushed past you in a crowd and you wouldn't have known your throat was cut until you went to nod your head and it rolled away down the street without you. I was the guy you were worrying about when you locked your doors and posted your guards and walked upstairs to bed, only to find me already up there before you, leaning on the dresser, just waiting in the dark.

I was the guy who always found a way.

I was the guy that couldn't be stopped.

But that's over now, I guess.

None of my stuff was original. I studied the best of the best, long ago. I learned from all of them. A move here, a move there, all stitched together. All the tricks. Including the greatest trick of all, which I learned from a man called Ryland. Back in the day Ryland worked all over, but mainly where there was oil, or white powder, or money, or girls, or high-stakes card games. Then he got old, and he slowly withdrew. Eventually he found the matrimonial market. Maybe he invented it, although I doubt that. But certainly he refined it. He turned it into a business. He was in the right place at the right time. Getting old and slowing down, just when all those California lawyers made divorce into a lottery win. Just when guys all over the hemisphere started to get nervous about it.

The theory was simple: A live wife goes to a lawyer, but a dead wife goes nowhere. Except the cemetery. Problem solved. A dead wife attracts a certain level of attention from the police, of course, but Ryland moved in a world where a guy would be a thousand times happier to get a call from a cop than a divorce lawyer. Cops would have to pussyfoot around the grief issue, and there was a general assumption that when it came to IQ, cops were not the sharpest chisels in the box. Whereas lawyers were like razors. And, of course, part of the appeal of a guy like Ryland was that evidence was going to be very thin on the ground. No question, a wife dead at Ryland's hands was generally considered to be a lottery win in reverse.

He worked hard. Hit the microfilm and check it out. Check newspapers all over the States and Central and South America. Look at Europe, Germany, Italy, anyplace where there were substantial fortunes at stake. Look at how many women went missing. Look at how old they were, and how long they had been married. Then check the follow-up stories, the inside pages, the later paragraphs, and see how many hints there were about incipient marital strife. Check it out, and you'll see a pattern.

The cops saw it too, of course. But Ryland was a ghost. He had survived oil and dope and moneylending and hookers and gambling. No way was he going to get brought down by greedy husbands and bored wives. He flourished, and I bet his name was never written down in any cop's file. Not anywhere, not once. He was that good.

He was working back in the days when billionaires were rare. Back then, a hundred million was considered a threshold level. Below a hundred mil, you were poor. Above, you were respectable. People called a hundred mil a unit, and most of Ryland's clients were worth three or four units. And Ryland noticed something: rich husband, rich wife. The wives weren't rich in the sense their husbands were, of course. They didn't have units of their own. But they had spending cash. It stands to reason, Ryland said to me. Guys set them up with bank accounts and credit cards. Guys worth three or four units don't like to trouble themselves with trivia down at the six-figure level.

But the six-figure level was where Ryland worked.

And he noticed that the blood he was spilling was dripping all over minks and diamond chokers and Paris gowns and perforated leather seats in Mercedes Benzes. He started searching purses after a while. There were big checking balances in most of them, and platinum cards. He didn't steal anything, of course. That would have been fatal, and stupid, and Ryland wasn't stupid. Not stupid at all. But he was imaginative.

Or so he claimed.

Actually, I like to believe one of the women handed the idea to him. Maybe one a little feistier than normal. Maybe when it became clear what was about to transpire, she put in a counter-offer. That's how I like to think it all started. Maybe she said: "That rat bastard. I should pay you to off him instead." I know Ryland's ears would have pricked up at that. Anything involving payment would have gotten him interested. He would have run the calculation at the same hyperspeed he used for any calculation, from a bullet's trajectory to a risk assessment. He would have figured: This chick can afford a six-figure coat, so she can afford a six-figure hit.

Thus, the greatest trick of all.

Getting paid twice.

He told me about it after he got sick with cancer, and I took it as a kind of anointment. The nomination of an heir. The passing of the baton. He wanted me to be the new Ryland. That was okay with me. I also took it as a mute appeal not to let him linger and suffer. That was okay with me too. He was frail by then. He resisted the pillow like crazy, but the lights went out soon enough. And there it was. The old Ryland gone, and the new Ryland starting out with new energy.

First up was a stout forty-something from Essen in Germany. Married to a steel baron who had recently found her to be boring. A hundred grand in my pocket would save him a hundred million in hers. Classically, of course, you would hunt and strike before she ever knew you were on the planet. Previously, that would have been the hallmark of a job well done.

But not anymore.

I went with her to Gstaad. I didn't travel with her. I just showed up there the next day. Got to know her a little. She was a cow. I would have gladly killed her for free. But I didn't. I talked to her. I worked her around to the point where she said, "My husband thinks I'm too old." Then she looked up at me from under her lashes. It was the usual reassurance-seeking crap. She wanted me to say. "You? Too old? How could he think that about such a beautiful woman?"

But I didn't say that.

Instead, I said, "He wants to get rid of you."

She took it as a question. She answered, "Yes, I think he does."

I said, "No, I know he does. He offered me money to kill you."

Think about it. How was she going to react? No screaming. No running to the Swiss cops. Just utter stunned silence, under the weight of the biggest single surprise she could have heard. First, of course, the conceptual question: "You're an assassin?" She knew people like me existed. She had moved in her husband's world for a long time. Too long, according to him. Then eventually, of course, the inevitable inquiry: "How much did he offer you?"

Ryland had told me to exaggerate a little. In his opinion it gave the victims a little perverse pleasure to hear a big number. It gave them a last shot at feeling needed, in a backhanded way. They weren't wanted any more, but at least it was costing a lot to get rid of them. Status, of a sort.

"Two hundred thousand US dollars," I said.

The fat Essen bitch took that in and then started down the wrong road.

She said, "I could give you that not to."

"Wouldn't work for me," I said. "I can't leave a job undone. He would tell people, and my reputation would be shot. A guy like me, his reputation is all he's got."

Gstaad was a good place to be having the conversation. It was isolated and otherworldly. It was like there was just her and me on the planet. I sat beside her and tried to radiate sympathy. Like a dentist, maybe. When he has to drill a tooth. I'm sorry . . . but it's got to be done. Her anger built, a little slow, but it came. Eventually she got on the right road.

"You work for money," she said.

I nodded.

"You work for anyone who can pay the freight," she said.

"Like a taxicab," I said.

She said, "I'll pay you to kill him."

There was anger there, of course, but there were also financial considerations. They were forming slowly in her mind, a little vaguely, but basically they were the exact obverse of the considerations I had seen in the husband's mind a week previously. People like that, it comes down to just four words: all the money, mine.

She asked, "How much?"

"The same," I said. "Two hundred grand."

We were in Switzerland, which made the banking part easy. I stuck with her, supportive, and watched her get her fat pink paws on two hundred thousand US dollars, crisp new bills from some European country's central reserve. She gave them to me and started to explain where her husband would be, and when.

"I know where he is," I said. "I have a rendezvous set up. For me to get paid."

She giggled at the irony. Guaranteed access to the victim. She wasn't dumb. That was the single greatest strength of Ryland's idea.

We went for a walk, alone, on a snow-covered track rarely frequented by skiers. I killed her there by breaking her fat neck and leaving her in a position that suggested a slip and a fall. Then I took the train back to Essen and kept my rendezvous with the husband. Obviously he had gone to great lengths to keep our meetings secret. He was in a place he wouldn't normally go, alone and unobserved. I collected my fee and killed him too. A silenced .22, in the head. It was an article of faith for people like Ryland and me. If you get paid, you have to deliver.

So, two fees, and all those steel units cascading down to fractious heirs that would be calling me themselves, soon enough. All the money, mine.

It went on like that for two years. Check the microfilm. Check the papers. North America, Central, South, all over Europe. Cops in a lather about anarchists targeting rich couples. That was another strength of Ryland's idea. It rendered the motive inexplicable.

Then I got an offer from Brazil. I was kind of surprised. For some reason I imagined their divorce laws to be old-fashioned and traditional. I didn't think any Brazilian guy would need my kind of help. But someone reached out to me and I ended up face to face with a man who had big units from mineral deposits and an actress wife who was sleeping around. The guy was wounded about it. Maybe that's why he called me. He didn't strictly need to. But he wanted to.

He was rich and he was angry, so I doubled my usual fee. That was no problem. I explained how it would work. Payment after the event at a discreet location, satisfaction guaranteed. Then he told me his wife was going to be on a train, some kind of a long private club-car journey through the mountains. That was a problem. There are no banks on trains. So I decided to pass on Ryland's trick, just this one time. I would go the traditional single-ended route. The old way. I checked a map and saw that I could get on the train late and get off early. The wife would be dead in her sleeper when it rolled into Rio. I would be long gone by then.

It was comforting to think about working the old way, just for once.

I spotted her on the train and kept well back. But even from a distance I saw the ring on her finger. It was a gigantic rock. A diamond so big they probably ran out of carat numbers to measure it with.

That was a bank right there, on her finger.

Traceable, theoretically, but not through certain parts of Amsterdam or Johannesburg or Freetown, Sierra Leone. Potentially a problem at customs posts, but I could swallow it.

I moved up the train.

She was a very beautiful woman. Skin like lavender honey, long black hair that shone, eyes like pools. Long legs, a tiny waist, a rack that was popping out of her shirt. I took the armchair opposite her and said, "Hello." I figured a woman who sleeps around would at least give me a look. I have certain rough qualities. A few scars, the kind of unkempt appearance that suggests adventure. She didn't need money. She was married to it. Maybe all she needed was diversion.

It went well at first and I found a reason to move around the table and slide into the chair next to her. Then within an hour we were well into that train-journey thing where she was leaning left and I was leaning right and we were sharing intimacies over the rush of the wind and the clatter of the wheels. She talked about her marriage briefly and then changed the subject. I brought it back. I pointed to her ring and asked her about it. She spread her hand like a starfish and let me take a look.

"My husband gave it to me," she said.

"So he should," I said. "He's a lucky man."

"He's an angry man," she said. "I don't behave myself very well, I'm afraid."

I said nothing.

She said, "I think he wants to have me killed."

So there it was, the opening that was often so hard to work around to. I should have said, "He does," and opened negotiations. But I didn't.

She said, "I look at the men I meet and I wonder, is this the one?"

So then I got my mouth working and said, "This is the one."

"Really?" she said.

I nodded. "I'm afraid so."

"But I have insurance," she said.

She raised her hand again and all I saw was the diamond. Hard to blame myself, because the diamond was so big and the stiletto's blade was so slender. I really didn't see it at all. Wasn't aware of its existence until its tip went through my shirt and pierced my skin.

Then she leaned on it with surprising strength and weight. It was cold. And long. A custom piece. It went right through me and pinned me to the chair. She used the heel of her hand and butted it firmly into place. Then she used my tie to wipe the handle clean of prints.

"Goodbye," she said.

She got up and left me there. I was unable to move. An inch left or right would tear my insides out. I just sat and felt the spreading stain of blood reach my lap. I'm still sitting there, ten minutes later. Once I could have shot you in one ear and out the other from a thousand yards. Or I could have brushed past you in a crowd and you wouldn't have known your throat was cut until you went to nod your head and it rolled away down the street without you. I was the guy you were worrying about when you locked your doors and posted your guards and walked upstairs to bed, only to find me already up there before you, leaning on the dresser, just waiting in the dark.

I was the guy who always found a way.

I was the guy that couldn't be stopped.

But then I met Ryland.

And all that's over now.

# TEN KEYS

Mostly shit happens, but sometimes things fall in your lap, not often, but enough times to drop a rock on despair. But you can't start in with thoughts of redemption. That would be inappropriate. Such events are not about you. Things fall in your lap not because you're good, but because other people are bad. And stupid.

This guy walked into a bar, which sounds like the start of a joke, which was what it was, really, in every way. The bar was a no-name dive with a peeled-paint door and no sign outside. As such it was familiar to me and the guy and people like us. I was already inside, at a table I had used before. I saw the guy come in. I knew him in the sense that I had seen him around a few times and therefore he knew me too, because as long as we assume a certain amount of reciprocity in the universe he had seen me around the exact same number of times. I see him, he sees me. We weren't friends. I didn't know his name. Which I wouldn't expect to. A guy like that, any name he gives you is sure to be bullshit. And certainly any name I would have given him would have been bullshit. So what were we to each other? Vague acquaintances, I guess. Both close enough and distant enough that given the trouble he was in, I was the sort of guy he was ready to talk to. Like two Americans trapped in a foreign airport. You assume an intimacy that isn't really there, and it makes it easier to spill your guts. You say things you wouldn't say in normal circumstances. This guy certainly did. He sat down at my table and started in on a whole long story. Not immediately, of course. I had to prompt him.

I asked, "You OK?"

He didn't reply. I didn't press. It was like starting a car that had been parked for a month. You don't just hammer the key. You give it time to settle, so you don't flood the carburetor or whatever cars have now. You're patient. In my line of work, patience is a big virtue.

I asked, "You want a drink?"

"Heineken," the guy said.

Right away I knew he was distracted. A guy like that, you offer him a drink, he should ask for something expensive and amber in a squat glass. Not a beer. He wasn't thinking. He wasn't calculating. But I was.

An old girl in a short skirt brought two bottles of beer, one for him and one for me. He picked his up and took a long pull and set it back down and I saw him feel the first complex shift of our new social dynamic. I had bought him a drink, so he owed me conversation. He had accepted charity, so he owed himself a chance to re-up his status. I saw him rehearse his opening statement, which was going to tell me what a hell of a big player he was.

"It never gets any easier," he said.

He was a white guy, thin, maybe thirty-five years old, a little squinty, the product of too many generations of inbred hardscrabble hill people, his DNA baked down to nothing more than the essential components, arms, legs, eyes, mouth. He was an atom, adequate, but entirely interchangeable with ten thousand just like him.

"Tell me about it," I said, ruefully, like I understood his struggle.

"A man takes a chance," he said. "Tries to get ahead. Sometimes it works, sometimes it don't."

I said nothing.

"I started out muling," he said. "Way back. You know that?"

I nodded. No surprise. We were four miles from I-95, and everyone started out muling, hauling keys of coke up from Miami or Jax, all the way north to New York and Boston. Anyone with a plausible face and an inconspicuous automobile started out muling, a single key in the trunk the first time, then two, then five, then ten. Trust was earned and success was rewarded, especially if you could make the length of the New Jersey Turnpike unmolested. The Jersey State Troopers were the big bottleneck back then.

"Clean and clear every time," the guy said. "No trouble, ever."

"So you moved up," I said.

"Selling," he said.

I nodded again. It was the logical next step. He would have been told to take his plausible face and his inconspicuous automobile deep into certain destination neighborhoods and meet with certain local distributors directly. The chain would have become one link shorter. Fewer hands on the product, fewer hands on the cash, more speed, more velocity, a better vector, less uncertainty.

"Who for?" I asked.

"The Martinez brothers."

"I'm impressed," I said, and he brightened a little.

"I got to where I was dealing ten keys pure at a time," he said.

My beer was getting warm, but I drank a little of it anyway. I knew what was coming next.

"I was hauling the coke north and the money south," he said.

I said nothing.

"You ever seen that much cash?" he asked. "I mean, really *seen* it?"

"No," I said.

"You can barely even lift it. You could get a hernia, a box like that."

I said nothing.

"I was doing two trips a week," he said. "I was never off the road. I wore grooves in the pavement. And there were dozens of us."

"Altogether a lot of cash," I said, because he needed me to open the door to the next revelation. He needed me to understand. He needed my permission to proceed.

"Like a river," he said.

I said nothing.

"Well, hell," he said. "There was so much it meant nothing to them. How could it? They were drowning in it."

"A man takes a chance," I said.

The guy didn't reply. Not at first. I held up two fingers to the old girl in the short skirt and watched her put two new bottles of Heineken on a cork tray.

"I took some of it," the guy said.

The old girl gave us our new bottles and took our old ones away. I said *four imports* to myself, so I could check my tab at the end of the night. Everyone's a rip-off artist now.

"How much of it did you take?" I asked the guy.

"Well, all of it. All of what they get for ten keys."

"And how much was that?"

"A million bucks. In cash."

"OK," I said, enthusiastically, deferentially, like *Wow, you're the man.*

"And I kept the product too," he said.

I just stared at him.

"From Boston," he said. "Dudes up there are paranoid. They keep the cash and the coke in separate places. And the city's all dug up. The way the roads are laid out now it's easier to get paid first and deliver second. They trusted me to do that, after a time."

"But this time you picked up the cash and disappeared before you delivered the product."

He nodded.

"Sweet," I said.

"I told the Martinez boys I got robbed."

"Did they believe you?"

"Maybe not," he said.

"Problem," I said.

"But I don't see why," he said. "Not really. Like, how much cash have you got in your pocket, right now?"

"Two hundred and change," I said. "I was just at the ATM."

"So how would you feel if you dropped a penny and it rolled down the storm drain? A single lousy cent?"

"I wouldn't really give a shit," I said.

"Exactly. This is like a guy with two hundred in his pocket who loses a penny under the sofa cushion. How uptight is anyone going to be?"

"With these guys, it's not about the money," I said.

"I know," he said.

We went quiet and drank our beers. Mine felt gassy against my teeth. I don't know how his felt to him. He probably wasn't tasting it at all.

"They've got this other guy," he said. "Dude called Octavian. He's their investigator. And their enforcer. He's going to come for me."

"People get robbed," I said. "Shit happens."

"Octavian is supposed to be real scary. I've heard bad things."

"You were robbed. What can he do?"

"He can make sure I'm telling the truth, is what he can do. I've heard he has a way of asking questions that makes you want to answer."

"You stand firm, he can't get blood out of a rock."

"They showed me a guy in a wheelchair. Story was that Octavian had him walking on his knees up and down a gravel patch for a week. Walking on the beach, he calls it. The pain is supposed to be terrible. And the guy got gangrene afterward, lost his legs."

"Who is this Octavian guy?"

"I've never seen him."

"Is he another Colombian?"

"I don't know."

"Didn't the guy in the wheelchair say?"

"He had no tongue. Story is Octavian cut it out."

"You need a plan," I said.

"He could walk in here right now. And I wouldn't know."

"So you need a plan fast."

"I could go to LA."

"Could you?"

"Not really," the guy said. "Octavian would find me. I don't want to be looking over my shoulder the whole rest of my life."

I paused. Took a breath.

"People get robbed, right?" I said.

"It happens," he said. "It's not unknown."

"So you could pin it on the Boston people. Start a war up there. Take the heat off of yourself. You could come out of this like an innocent victim. The first casualty. Nearly a hero."

"If I can convince this guy Octavian."

"There are ways."

"Like what?"

"Just convince yourself first. You were the victim here. If you really believe it, in your mind, this guy Octavian will believe it too. Like acting a part."

"It won't go easy."

"A million bucks is worth the trouble. Two million, assuming you're going to sell the ten keys."

"I don't know."

"Just stick to a script. You know nothing. It was the Boston guys. Whoever he is, Octavian's job is to get results, not to waste his time

29

down a blind alley. You stand firm, and he'll tell the Martinez boys you're clean and they'll move on."

"Maybe."

"Just learn a story and stick to it. *Be* it. Method acting, like that fat guy who just died."

"Marlon Brando?"

"That's the one. Do like him. You'll be OK."

"Maybe."

"But Octavian will search your crib."

"That's for damn sure," the guy said. "He'll tear it apart."

"So the stuff can't be there."

"It *isn't* there."

"That's good," I said, and then I lapsed into silence.

"What?" he asked.

"Where is it?" I asked.

"I'm not going to tell you," he said.

"That's OK," I said. "I don't want to know. Why the hell would I? But the thing is, you can't afford to know, either."

"How can I not know?"

"That's the exact problem," I said. "This guy Octavian's going to see it in your eyes. He's going to see you *knowing*. He's going to be beating up on you or whatever and he needs to see a blankness in your eyes. Like you don't have a clue. That's what he needs to see. But he isn't going to see that."

"What's he going to see?"

"He's going to see you holding out and thinking, Hey, tomorrow this will be over and I'll be back at my cabin or my storage locker or wherever and then I'll be OK. He's going to *know*."

"So what should I do?"

I finished the last of my beer. Warm, and flat. I considered ordering two more but I didn't. I figured we were near the end. I figured I didn't need any more of an investment.

"Maybe you should go to LA," I said.

"No," he said.

"So you should let me hold the stuff for you. Then you genuinely won't know where it is. You're going to need that edge."

"I'd be nuts. Why should I trust you?"

"You shouldn't. You don't have to."

"You could disappear with my two million."

"I could, but I won't. Because if I did, you'd call Octavian and tell him that a face just came back to you. You'd describe me, and then your problem would become my problem. And if Octavian is as bad as you say, that's a problem I don't want."

"You better believe it."

"I do believe it."

"Where would I find you afterward?"

"Right here," I said. "You know I use this place. You've seen me in here before."

"Method acting," he said.

"You can't betray what you don't know," I said.

He went quiet for a long time. I sat still and thought about putting one million dollars in cash and ten keys of uncut cocaine in the trunk of my car.

"OK," he said.

"There would be a fee," I said, to be plausible.

"How much?" he asked.

"Fifty grand," I said.

He smiled.

"OK," he said again.

"Like a penny under the sofa cushion," I said.

"You got that right."

"We're all winners."

The bar door opened and a guy walked in on a blast of warm air. Hispanic, small and wide, big hands, an ugly scar high on his cheek.

"You know him?" my new best friend asked.

"Never saw him before," I said.

The new guy walked to the bar and sat on a stool.

"We should do this thing right now," my new best friend said.

Sometimes, things just fall in your lap.

"Where's the stuff?" I asked.

"In an old trailer in the woods," he said.

"Is it big?" I asked. "I'm new to this."

"Ten kilos is twenty-two pounds," the guy said. "About the same for the money. Two duffels, is all."

"So let's go," I said.

I drove him in my car west and then south and he directed me down a fire road and onto a dirt track that led to a clearing. I guessed once it had been neat, but now it was overgrown with all kinds of stuff and it stank of animal piss and the trailer had degenerated from a viable vacation home to a rotted hulk. It was all covered over with mold and mildew and the windows were dark with organic scum. He wrestled with the door and went inside. I opened the trunk lid and waited. He came back out with a duffle in each hand. Carried them over to me.

"Which is which?" I asked.

He squatted down and unzipped them. One had bricks of used money, the other had bricks of dense white powder packed hard and smooth under clear plastic wrap.

"OK," I said.

He stood up again and heaved the bags into the trunk and I stepped to the side and shot him twice in the head. Birds rose up from everywhere and cawed and cackled and settled back into the branches. I put the gun back in my pocket and took out my cell phone. Dialed a number.

"Yes?" the Martinez brothers asked, both together. They always used the speakerphone. They were too afraid of each other's betrayal to allow private calls.

"This is Octavian," I said. "I'm through here. I got the money back and I took care of the guy."

"Already?"

"I got lucky," I said. "It fell in my lap."

"What about the ten keys?"

"In the wind," I said. "Long gone."

# SAFE ENOUGH

Wolfe was a city boy. From birth his world had been iron and concrete, first one city block, then two, then four, then eight. Trees had been visible only from the roof of his building, far away across the East River, as remote as legends. Until he was twenty-eight years old the only mown grass he had ever seen was the outfield at Yankee Stadium. He was oblivious to the chlorine taste of city water, and to him the roar of traffic was the same thing as absolute tranquil silence.

Now he lived in the country.

Anyone else would have called it the suburbs, but there were broad spaces between dwellings, and no way of knowing what your neighbor was cooking other than getting invited to dinner, and there was insect life in the yards, and wild deer, and the possibility of mice in the basement, and drifts of leaves in the fall, and electricity came through wires slung on poles and water came from wells.

To Wolfe, that was the country.

That was the wild frontier.

That was the end of a long and winding road.

The road had started winding twenty-three years earlier in a Bronx public elementary school. Back in those rudimentary days a boy was marked early. Hooligan, wastrel, artisan, genius, the label was slapped firmly in place and it stuck forever. Wolfe had been reasonably well behaved and had managed shop and arithmetic pretty well, so he was stuck in the artisan category and expected to grow up to be a plumber or an electrician or an air-conditioning guy. He was expected to find a sponsor in the appropriate local and get admitted to an apprenticeship and then work for forty-five years. Which is precisely how it turned out for Wolfe. He went the electrician route and was ten years into his allotted forty-five when it happened.

What happened was that the construction boom in the suburbs finally overwhelmed the indigenous supply of father-and-son electrical contractors. That was all they had up there. Small guys, family firms, one-truck operations, mom doing the invoices. Same for the local roofers and plumbers and drywall people. Demand outran supply. But the developers had bucks to make and couldn't tolerate delay. So they swallowed their pride and sent flyers down to the city union halls, and followed them with minivans, pick up at seven in the morning, back in time for dinner. They found it easy to compete on wages. City budgets were stalled.

Wolfe was not the first to sign up, but he wasn't the last. Every morning at seven o'clock he would climb into a Dodge Caravan full of stuff belonging to some suburban foreman's kids. A bunch of other city guys would climb in behind him. They would stay silent and morose through the one-hour trip, but they watched out the windows with a degree of curiosity. Some of them were turned out early in a manicured town full of quarter-acre lots. Some of them stayed in until the trees thickened up and they hit the north of the county.

Wolfe was put to work on the last stop up the line.

Anyone who had seen a little more geography than Wolfe would have pegged the place correctly as mildly undulating terrain covered with hundred-year-old second-growth forestation and a few glacial boulders, with some minor streams and some small ponds. Wolfe thought it was the Rocky Mountains. To him, it was unbelievably dramatic. Birds sang and chipmunks darted and there was gray lichen on the rocks and tangled riots of vines everywhere.

His worksite was a stick-built wooden house going up on a nine-acre lot. Every conceivable thing was different from the city. There was raw mud under his feet. Power came in on a cable as thick as his wrist that was spliced off another looping between two tarred poles on the shoulder of the road. The new feed was terminated at a meter and a breaker box screwed to a plyboard that was set upright in the earth like a gravestone. It was a 200-amp supply. It ran underground in a graveled trench the length of the future driveway, which was about as long as the Grand Concourse. Then it came out in the future basement, through a patched wound in the concrete foundation.

Then it was Wolfe's to deal with.

He worked alone most of the time. Drywall crews were scarce. Nobody was slated to show up until he was finished. Then they would blitz the Sheetrock job and move on. So Wolfe was a small cog in a big dispersed machine. He was happy enough about that. It was easy work. And pleasant. He liked the smell of the raw lumber. He liked the ease of drilling wooden studs with an auger instead of fighting through brick or concrete with a hammer. He liked the way he could stand up most of the time, instead of crawling. He liked the fresh cleanliness of the site. Better than poking around in piles of old rat shit.

He grew to like the area, too.

Every day he brought a bag lunch from a deli at home. At first he ate in what was going to be the garage, sitting on a plank. Then he took to venturing out and sitting on a rock. Then he found a better rock, near a stream. Then he found a place across the stream with two rocks, one like a table and the other like a chair.

Then he found a woman.

She was walking through the woods, fast. Vines whipped at her legs. He saw her, but she didn't see him. She was preoccupied. Angry, or upset. She looked like a spirit of the countryside. A goddess of the forest. She was tall, she was straight, she had untamed straw-blonde hair, she wore no makeup. She had what magazines call bone structure. She had blue eyes and pale delicate hands.

Later, from the foreman, Wolfe learned that the lot he was working on had been her land. She had sold nine of thirty acres for development. Wolfe also learned that her marriage was in trouble. Local scuttlebutt said that her husband was an asshole. He was a Wall Street guy who commuted on Metro-North. Never home, and when he was he gave her a hard time. Story was he had tried to stop her selling the nine acres, but the land was hers. Story was they fought all the time, in that tight-ass half-concealed way that respectable people use. The husband had been heard to say "I'll f-ing kill you" to her. She was a little more buttoned-up, but the story was she had said it right back.

Suburban gossip was amazingly extensive. Where Wolfe was from, you didn't need gossip. You heard everything through the walls.

They gave Wolfe time and a half to work Saturdays and slipped him big bills to run phone lines and cable. Being a union man, he shouldn't have done it. But there were going to be modems, and a media room, and five bedroom phone extensions sharing three lines. Plus fax. Plus a DSL option. So he took the money and did the work.

He saw the woman most days.

She didn't see him.

He learned her routine. She had a green Volvo wagon and he would see it pass the bottom of the new driveway when she went to the store. One day he saw it go and downed tools and walked through the woods and stepped over the property line onto her land. Walked where she had walked. The trees were dense, but after about twenty yards he came out on a broad lawn that led up to her house. The first time, he stopped there, right on the edge.

The second time, he went a little farther.

By the fifth time, he had been all over her property. He had explored everything. He had taken his shoes off and padded through her kitchen. She didn't lock her door. Nobody did, in the suburbs. It was a badge of distinction. "We never lock our doors," they all said, with a little laugh.

More fool them.

Wolfe finished the furnace line in the new basement and started on the first floor. Every day he took his lunch to the twin rocks. One time-and-a-half Saturday he saw the woman and her husband together. They were on their lawn, fighting. Not physically. Verbally. They were striding up and down the grass in the hot sunlight and Wolfe saw them between tree branches like they were on a stage under a flashing stroboscope. Like disco. Fast sequential poses of anger and hurt. The guy was an asshole, for sure. Completely unreasonable, in Wolfe's estimation. The more he railed, the lovelier the woman looked. Like a martyr in a church window. Wounded, vulnerable, noble.

Then the asshole hit her.

It was a kind of girly roundhouse slap. Try that where Wolfe was from and your opponent would laugh for a minute before beating you to a pulp. But it worked well enough on the woman. The asshole was tall and fleshy and he got enough of his dumb bulk behind the blow to lift her off her feet and dump her on her back on the grass. She sat up, stunned. Disbelieving. There was a livid red mark on her cheek. She started to cry. Not tears of pain. Not even tears of rage. Just tears of sheer heartbroken sadness that whatever great things her life had promised, it had all come down to being dumped on her ass on her own back lawn, with four fingers and a thumb printed backward on her face.

Soon after that it was the Fourth of July weekend and Wolfe stayed at home for four days.

———

When the Dodge Caravan brought him back again he saw a bunch of local cop cars coming down the road. From the woman's house, probably. No flashing lights. He glanced at them twice and started work. Second floor, three lighting circuits. Switched outlets and ceiling fixtures. Wall sconces in the bathrooms. But the whine of his auger must have told the woman he was there because she came over to see him. First time she had actually laid eyes on him. As far as he knew. Certainly it was the first time they had talked.

She crunched her way over the driveway grit and leaned in past the plywood sheet that was standing in for the front door and called, "Hello?"

Wolfe heard her over the noise of the drill and clattered down the stairs. She had stepped inside the hallway. The light was behind her. It made a halo of her hair. She was wearing old jeans and a T-shirt. She was a vision of loveliness.

"I'm sorry to bother you," she said.

Her voice was like an angel's caress.

Wolfe said, "No bother."

"My husband has disappeared," she said.

"Disappeared?" Wolfe said.

"He wasn't home over the weekend and he isn't at work today."

Wolfe said nothing.

The woman said, "The police will come to see you. I'm here to apologize for that in advance. That's all, really."

But Wolfe could tell it wasn't.

"Why would the police come to see me?" he asked.

"I think they'll have to. I think that's how they do things. They'll probably want to know if you saw anything. Or heard any . . . disturbances."

The way she said disturbances was really a question, real-time, from her to him, not just a future prediction of what the cops might ask. Like, Did you hear the disturbances? Did you? Or not?

Wolfe said, "My name is Wolfe. I'm pleased to meet you."

The woman said, "I'm Mary. Mary Lovell."

Lovell. Like love, with two extra letters.

"Did you hear anything, Mr. Wolfe?"

"No," Wolfe said. "I'm just working here. Making a bit of noise myself."

"It's just that the police are being a bit . . . distant. I know that if a wife disappears, the police always suspect the husband. Until something is proven otherwise. I'm wondering if they're wondering the same kind of thing, but in reverse."

Wolfe said nothing.

"Especially if there have been disturbances," Mary Lovell said.

"I didn't hear anything," Wolfe said.

"Especially if the wife isn't very upset."

"Aren't you upset?"

"I'm a little sad. Sad that I'm happy."

———

Sure enough the police came by about two hours later. Two of them. Town cops, in uniform. Wolfe guessed the department wasn't big enough to carry detectives. The cops approached him politely and told him a long and rambling story that basically recapped the local gossip. Husband and wife on the outs, always fighting, famous for it. They said up-front and man to man that if the wife had disappeared they'd have some serious questions for the husband. The other way around was unusual but not unknown and, frankly, the town was full of rumors. So, they asked, could Mr. Wolfe shed any light?

No, Mr. Wolfe said, he couldn't.

"Never seen them?" the first cop asked.

"I guess I've seen her," Wolfe said. "In her car, time to time. Leastways, I'm guessing it was her. Right direction."

"Green Volvo?"

"That was it."

"Never seen him?" the second cop asked.

"Never," Wolfe said. "I'm just here working."

"Ever heard anything?"

"Like what?"

"Like fights, or altercations."

"Not a thing."

The first cop said, "This is a guy who apparently walked away from a big career in the city. And guys don't do that. They get lawyers instead."

"What can I tell you?"

"We're just saying."

"Saying what?"

"The load bed on that Volvo is seven feet long, you put the seats down."

"So?"

"It would help us to hear that you didn't happen to look out the window and see that Volvo drive past with something maybe six-three long, maybe wrapped up in a rug or a sheet of plastic."

"I didn't."

"She's known to have uttered threats. Him too. I'm telling you, if she was gone, we'd be looking at him, for sure."

Wolfe said nothing.

The cop said, "Therefore we have to look at her. We have to be sensitive about equality. It's forced on us."

The cop looked at Wolfe one last time, working man to working man, appealing for class solidarity, hoping for a break.

But Wolfe just said, "I'm working here. I don't see things."

---

Wolfe saw cop cars up and down the road all day long. He didn't go home that night. He let the Dodge Caravan leave without him and went over to Mary Lovell's house.

He said, "I came by to see how you're doing."

She said, "They think I killed him."

She led him inside to the kitchen he had visited before.

She said, "They have witnesses who heard me make threats. But they were meaningless. Just things you say in fights."

"Everyone says those things," Wolfe said.

"But it's really his job they're worried about. They say nobody just walks away from a job like his. And they're right. And if somebody did, they'd use a credit card for a plane or a hotel. And he hasn't. So what's he doing? Using cash in a fleabag motel somewhere? Why would he do that? That's what they're harping on."

Wolfe said nothing.

Mary Lovell said, "He's just disappeared. It's impossible to explain."

Wolfe said nothing.

Mary Lovell said, "I would suspect myself too. I really would."

"Is there a gun in the house?" Wolfe asked.

"No," Mary said.

"Kitchen knives all accounted for?"

"Yes."

"So how do they think you did it?"

"They haven't said."

"They've got nothing," Wolfe said.

Then he went quiet.

Mary said, "What?"

Wolfe said, "I saw him hit you."

"When?"

"Before the holidays. I was in the woods, you were on the lawn."

"You watched us?"

"I saw you. There's a difference."

"Did you tell the police?"

"No."

"Why not?"

"I wanted to talk to you first."

45

"About what?"

"I wanted to ask you a question."

"What question?"

"Did you kill him?"

There was a tiny pause, hardly there at all, and then Mary Lovell said, "No."

---

It started that night. They felt like conspirators. Mary Lovell was the kind of suburban avant-garde bohemian that didn't let herself dismiss an electrician from the Bronx out of hand. And Wolfe had nothing against upscale women. Nothing at all.

---

Wolfe never went home again. The first three months were tough. Taking a new lover five days after her husband was last seen alive made things worse for Mary Lovell. Obviously. Much worse. The rumor mill started up full blast and the cops never left her alone. But she got through it. At night, with Wolfe, she was fine. The tiny seed of doubt that she knew had to be in his mind bound her to him. He never mentioned it. He was always unfailingly loyal. It made her feel committed to him, unquestioningly, like a fact of life. Like she was a princess and had been promised to someone at birth. That she liked him just made it better.

---

After three months the cops moved on, mentally. The Lovell husband's file gathered dust as an unsolved case. The rumor mill quieted. In a year it was ancient history. Mary and Wolfe got along fine. Life was good. Wolfe set up as a one-man contractor. Worked for the local developers out of a truck that Mary bought for him. She did the invoices.

———

It soured before their third Christmas. Finally Mary admitted to herself that beyond the bohemian attraction her electrician from the Bronx was a little . . . boring. He didn't know anything. And his family was a pack of wild animals. And the fact that she was bound to him by the tiny seed of doubt that had to be in his mind became a source of resentment, not charm. She felt that far from being clandestine coconspirators they were now cell-mates in a prison constructed by her long-forgotten husband.

For his part Wolfe was getting progressively more and more irritated by her. She was so damn snooty about everything. So smug, so superior. She didn't like baseball. And she said even if she did, she wouldn't root for the Yankees. They just bought everything. Like she didn't?

He began to sympathize vaguely with the long-forgotten husband. One time he replayed the slap on the lawn in his mind. The long sweep of the guy's arm, the arc of his hand. He imagined the rush of air on his own palm and the sharp sting that would come as contact was made.

Maybe she had deserved it.

One time face to face in the kitchen he found his own arm moving in the same way. He checked it inside a quarter-inch. Mary never noticed. Maybe she was shaping up to hit him. It seemed only a matter of time.

The third Christmas was where it fell apart. Or to be accurate, the aftermath of the third Christmas. The holiday itself was OK. Just. Afterward she was prissy. As usual. In the Bronx you had fun and then you threw the tree on the sidewalk. But she always waited until January 6th and planted the tree in the yard.

"Shame to waste a living thing," she would say.

The trees she made him buy had roots. He had never before seen a Christmas tree with roots. To him, it was all wrong. It spoke of foresight, and concern for the long-term, and some kind of guilt-ridden self-justification. Like you were permitted to have fun only if you did the right thing afterward. It wasn't like that in Wolfe's world. In Wolfe's world, fun was fun. No before, and no after.

Planting a tree to her was cutesy. To him it was a backbreaking hour digging in the freezing cold.

They fought about it, of course. Long, loud, and hard. Within seconds it was all about class and background and culture. Furious insults were thrown. The air grew thick with them. They kept on until they were physically too tired to continue. Wolfe was shaken. She had reached in and touched a nerve. Touched his core: No woman should speak to a man like that. He knew it was an ignoble feeling. He knew it was wrong, out of date, too traditional for words.

But he was what he was.

He looked at her and in that moment he knew he hated her.

He found his gloves and wrapped himself up in his down coat and seized the tree by a branch and hurled it out the back door. Detoured via the garage and seized a shovel. Dragged the tree behind him to a spot at the edge of the lawn, under the shade of a giant maple, where the snow was thin and the damn Christmas tree would be sure to die. He kicked leaf litter and snow out of his way and plunged the shovel into the earth. Hurled clods deep into the woods. Cut maple roots with vicious stabs. After ten minutes sweat was rolling down his back. After fifteen minutes the hole was two feet deep.

After twenty minutes he saw the first bone.

He fell to his knees. Swept dirt away with his hands. The thing was dirty white, long, shaped like the kind of thing you gave a dog in a cartoon show. There were stringy dried ligaments attached to it and rotted cotton cloth surrounding it.

Wolfe stood up. Turned slowly and stared at the house. Walked toward it. Stopped in the kitchen. Opened his mouth.

"Come to apologize?" Mary said.

Wolfe turned away. Picked up the phone.

Dialed 911.

———

The locals called the state troopers. Mary was kept under some kind of unofficial house arrest in the kitchen until the excavation was completed. A state lieutenant showed up with a search warrant. One of his men pulled an old credenza away from the garage wall and found a hammer behind it. A carpentry tool.

Dried blood and old hair were still clearly visible on it. It was bagged up and carried out to the yard. The profile of its head exactly matched the hole punched through the skull they had found in the ground.

At that point Mary Lovell was arrested for the murder of her husband.

———

Then science took over. Dental, blood, and DNA tests proved the remains to be those of the husband. No question about that. It was the husband's blood and hair on the hammer, too. No question about that, either. Mary's fingerprints were on the hammer's handle. Twenty-three points of similarity, more than enough for the locals, the state police, and the FBI all put together.

———

Then lawyers took over. The county DA loved the case to bits. To put a middle-class white woman away would prove his impartial evenhandedness. Mary got a lawyer, the friend of a friend. He was good, but overmatched. Not by the DA. By the weight of evidence. Mary wanted to plead not guilty, but he persuaded her to say yes to manslaughter. Emotional turmoil, temporary loss of reason, everlasting regret and remorse. So one day in late spring Wolfe sat in the courtroom and watched her go down for a minimum ten years. She looked at him only once during the whole proceeding.

Then Wolfe went back to her house.

——

He lived there alone for many years. He kept on working and did his own invoices. He grew to really love the solitude and the silence. Sometimes he drove down to the Stadium but when parking hit twenty bucks he figured his Bronx days were over. He bought a big-screen TV. Did his own cable work, of course. Watched the games at home. Sometimes after the last out he would sit in the dark and review the case in his head. Cops, lawyers, dozens of them. They had done a pretty thorough job between them.

But they had missed two vital questions.

One: With her pale delicate hands, how was Mary Lovell accustomed to handling hammers and shovels? Why did the local cops right at the beginning not see angry red blisters all over her palms?

And two: How did Wolfe know exactly where to start digging the hole for that damn Christmas tree? Right after the fight? Aren't cops supposed to hate coincidences?

But all in all Wolfe figured he was safe enough.

# NORMAL IN EVERY WAY

In 1954, the San Francisco Police Department was as good or as bad as any other large urban force in the nation. Which is to say it was mixed. It was part noble, part diligent, part grudgingly dutiful, part lazy and defensive, part absurdly corrupt, and abusive, and violent. In other words normal in every way. Including in the extent of its resources. Now they seem pitifully few. Then they were all there was. Manual typewriters and carbon paper, files in cardboard boxes, and old rotary dial telephones, sitting up straight and proud on metal war surplus desks.

It goes without saying there were no computers. There were no databases. No search engines. No keywords or metadata. No automatic matching. All there was were men in a room. With fallible memories. Some of them drank. Most of them, in fact. Some put more effort into forgetting than remembering. Such were the times. The result was each new crime was in danger of standing alone, entire unto itself. Links and chimes and resonances with previous crimes were in danger of going unheard.

All police departments were in the same boat. Not just San Francisco. Every one of them evolved the same de facto solution. Separately and independently, fumbling blind, but they all ended up in the same place. The file clerk became the font of all wisdom. Usually a grizzled old veteran, sometimes confined to a desk due to getting shot or beaten, presiding over a basement emporium packed with furred old file folders and bulging old boxes on shelves. Usually he had been there many years. Usually he chatted and gossiped and remembered things. Sometimes he knew a guy who knew a guy, in another part of town. He became a database, as imperfect as it was, and the guys who knew guys became a network, even though partial and patchy. Carbon-based information technology. Not silicon. All there was. The same everywhere.

Except in one station in San Francisco the file clerk was not a grizzled old veteran. He was a misfit rookie by the name of Walter Kleb. He wasn't much more than a kid at the time. He was shy and awkward and strange in his mannerisms. He didn't stutter or stammer but sometimes he would need to try out a whole sentence in his head, maybe even to rehearse it on his lips, before he could speak it out loud. He was considered odd. Retarded for sure. A screw loose. Nuts, psycho, spastic, crazy, loony, schizo, freak. In 1954 there was no better vocabulary for such things. He struggled through the academy. He was hopeless in most ways, but his paper grades were sky-high. Never been seen before. No one could figure out how to get rid of him. Eventually he was assigned to duty.

He showed up wearing an overstarched uniform too big in the neck. He was an embarrassment. He made it to the file room in record time. No long previous career. No shooting or beating. But he was happy in the basement. He was alone most of the time. With nothing to do except read and learn and alphabetize and arrange in date order. Occasionally people came to see him, and they were politer than most, and kinder, because they wanted something. Either to return a file, or take one out, maybe without anyone knowing, or to find something that had been accidently lost, or to lose something that had been inadvertently found.

What none of them did was ask database questions. Why would they? How could a retard rookie who had only been there five minutes know anything? Which was a shame, Kleb thought, because he did know things. The reading and the learning were producing results. True, he had no network of guys who knew guys. That strength was certainly deficient. He wasn't a boy who could call up a grizzled old veteran a precinct away and gossip for twenty minutes on the phone. Or ask a favor. Or do one. He wasn't that boy at all. But he was a boy who made lists and liked connections and enjoyed anomalies. He felt they should have asked him questions. Of course he never spoke up first. Well, except for once. Late in January. And look what happened after that.

A detective named Cleary came down and asked for a file nearly a year old. Kleb knew it. He had read it. It was an unsolved homicide. Thought likely to be political. Conceivably at the secret agent level. There were certain interesting factors.

Kleb asked, "Has there been a break in the case?"

Cleary looked like he had been slapped. At first Kleb thought not slapped as in insulted, but just astonished, that the retard spoke, and showed awareness, and asked a question. Then he realized no, slapped as in rudely jerked from one train of thought to another. Cleary's mind had been somewhere else. Not thinking about breaks in the old case. The only other reason for getting the file was therefore a new case. With similarities, possibly.

In the end Cleary took the file and walked away without a word. Kleb was forced to reconstruct its contents in his head. Homicide by gunshot, apparently at very long range. The victim was an immigrant from the Soviet Union. He was thought to be either a reformed communist gunned down as a punishment by an actual communist, or the reform was fake and he was really a sleeper agent, taken care of by a shadowy outfit with a deniable office close to the inner ring of the Pentagon. In 1954 either theory was entirely plausible.

As always at lunch Kleb sat alone, but that day one table closer to the crowd, to better hear what they were saying. The new case was a baffler. A Soviet immigrant, shot with a rifle from far away. No one knew why. Probably a spy. Then someone said no, State Department back channels were reporting no sensitivity. Therefore no spies involved. Just regular folk, doing whatever regular folk do, with deer rifles in Golden Gate Park.

Kleb went back to the basement, and back inside his head. He read the first file all over again. He checked every detail. He weighed every aspect. The date of the crime, January 31, 1953, exactly 361 days earlier, the location, also Golden Gate Park, a lonely time of day, few potential witnesses, zero actual witnesses. Bullet fragments suggested a medium caliber high-velocity rifle round. A disturbed patch of dirt behind a tree five hundred yards away was thought to be where it was fired from.

Cleary came back again early in the afternoon.

"You asked me a question," he said.

Kleb nodded, but didn't speak.

Cleary said, "You knew it was an unsolved case."

Again Kleb nodded, but didn't speak.

"You read the file."

"Yes," Kleb said.

"You read all the files."

"Yes," Kleb said again.

"We got anything else like this?"

A database question.

His first.

"No," Kleb said.

"Pity."

"But the two cases are very like each other."

"Why I hoped there might be a third."

Kleb said, "I think the five-hundred-yard range is important."

"You a detective now?"

"No, but I notice patterns. There have been many gunshot homicides in the park. Almost all of them have been close range.

Easier to walk right up to someone on a twisty path. Long-distance rifle fire is a large anomaly. It would suggest a strong preference. Or familiarity. Or possibly training. Maybe that's the only way he knows how to do it."

"You think he's ex-military?"

"I think it's likely."

"So do I, Einstein. Between World War Two and Korea, half the population is ex-military. That would cover everyone from a hobo living under a bridge to the hot boys working for the back offices in the Pentagon. The President of the United States is ex-military. Ex-military gets us precisely nowhere. Keep thinking, genius. That's what you're good at."

"Is there a connection between the victims?"

"Other than being commies?" Cleary said.

"Were they?"

"They claimed not to be. They spoke out from time to time. They had nothing else in common. They had never met and as far as we can tell never knew about each other."

"That's how it would look, if they were spies."

"Exactly," Cleary said.

"Also how it would look if they weren't."

"Therefore this line of inquiry gets us precisely nowhere, either. Keep thinking, brainbox."

"How would you describe being a Soviet immigrant and a reformed communist?"

"How would I describe it?" Cleary said. "Smart."

"But difficult," Kleb said. "Don't you think? You would have to work at it. Frequent reaffirmations would be expected. As you said, they spoke out from time to time. They must have achieved a small degree of local notoriety."

"Does this matter?"

"I wondered how the shooter identified them as Russians from five hundred yards."

"Maybe being Russians was a coincidence. Maybe they were just walkers in the park. Targets of convenience."

"Not a well-represented national origin here. The odds are against it. But it's certainly possible. Although I feel somehow it shouldn't be. It's almost a philosophical inquiry."

"What is?"

Kleb tested a sentence in his head, and then on his lips. Out loud he said, "There's a second issue that might or might not be a coincidence. Is it too big of a coincidence that two other things might or might not be coincidences also? Or do all three things reinforce each other and make the implication more likely to be true than false? It's an existential question."

"Speak English, loony boy."

"I think the dates might be important. They might explain the Russians. Or not, of course, if it's all just one big coincidence. Then my theory collapses like a house of cards."

"What dates?"

"The dates of the shootings. January 31, 1953, and today, which is January 27, 1954."

"What do they have in common?"

Kleb tested another sentence in his head, and on his lips. It was a long sentence. It felt okay. Out loud he said, "I think you should look for a German national in his thirties. Almost certainly a local resident. Almost certainly an ex-prisoner of war, detained back in Kansas or Iowa or somewhere. Almost certainly an infantryman, likely a sniper. Almost certainly married a local girl and stayed here. But he never gave up the faith. He never stopped believing. Certain things upset him. Like January 31, 1953."

"Why would it?"

"It was the tenth anniversary of the Germans' final surrender at Stalingrad. January 31, 1943. Their first defeat. Catastrophic. It was the beginning of the end. Our believer wanted to strike back. He found a Red in the neighborhood. Maybe he had heard him speak at the Legion Hall. He shot him in the park."

"The date could be a total coincidence."

"Then today would have to be, too. That's what I'm trying to figure out. Does the fact that the dates could be significant together mean they must be?"

"What's today?"

"The tenth anniversary of the lifting of the siege of Leningrad. Another catastrophic retreat for the Germans. Another huge symbolic failure. Stalin, Lenin. Their cities survived. Our believer didn't like it."

"How many more anniversaries are coming up?"

"Thick and fast now," Kleb said. "It was Armageddon from this point onward. The fall of Berlin comes on the second of May next year."

Cleary was quiet a long moment.

Then he winked.

He said, "You keep thinking, smart boy. That's what you're good at."

Then he walked away.

Late the next day Kleb heard Cleary had ordered a sudden change of direction for the investigation, which paid off almost right away. They made an arrest almost immediately. A German national, aged thirty-four, a local resident, an ex-prisoner of war who had been held in Kansas, previously a sniper with an elite division, now married to a Kansas woman and living in California. Cleary got a medal and a commendation and his name in the paper. Never once did he mention Kleb's help. Even to Kleb himself. Which turned out to be representative. Kleb worked forty-six years in that basement, shy, awkward, strange in his mannerisms, largely ignored, largely avoided, and by his own objective count provided material assistance in forty-seven separate cases. An average of more than one a year, just. He was never thanked and never recognized. He retired without gifts or speeches or a party, but nevertheless it was a happy day for him, because it was the anniversary of the moon landing, which meant, same day, different year, it was also the anniversary of the first vehicle on Mars. Which was the kind of connection he liked.

# THE .50 SOLUTION

M ost times I assess the client and then the target and only afterward do I set the price. It's about common sense and variables.
If the client is rich, I ask for more. If the target is tough, I ask for
more. If there are major expenses involved, I ask for more. So if
I'm working overseas on behalf of a billionaire against a guy in a
remote hideout with a competent protection team on his side, I'm
going to ask for maybe a hundred times what I would want from
some local chick looking to solve her marital problems in a quick
and messy manner. Variables, and common sense.

But this time the negotiation started differently.

The guy who came to see me was rich. That was clear. His
wealth was pore-deep. Not just his clothes. Not just his car. This

was a guy who had been rich forever. Maybe for generations. He was tall and gray and silvery and self-assured. He was a patrician. It was all right there in the way he held himself, the way he spoke, the way he took charge.

First thing he talked about was the choice of weapon.

He said, "I hear you've used a Barrett Model Ninety on more than one occasion."

I said, "You hear right."

"You like that piece?"

"It's a fine rifle."

"So you'll use it for me."

"I choose the weapon," I said.

"Based on what?"

"Need."

"You'll need it."

I asked, "Why? Long range?"

"Maybe two hundred yards."

"I don't need a Barrett Ninety for two hundred yards."

"It's what I want."

"Will the target be wearing body armor?"

"No."

"Inside a vehicle?"

"Open air."

"Then I'll use a three-oh-eight. Or something European."

"I want that fifty-caliber shell."

"A three-oh-eight or a NATO round will get him just as dead from two hundred yards."

"Maybe not."

Looking at him I was pretty sure this was a guy who had never fired a .50 Barrett in his life. Or a .308 Remington. Or an M16, or an FN, or an H & K. Or any kind of a rifle. He had probably never fired anything at all, except maybe a BB gun as a kid and workers as an adult.

I said, "The Barrett is an awkward weapon. It's four feet long and it doesn't break down. It weighs twenty-two pounds. It's got bipod legs, for Christ's sake. It's like an artillery piece. Hard to conceal. And it's very loud. Maybe the loudest rifle in the history of the world."

He said, "I like that fifty-caliber shell."

"I'll give you one," I said. "You can plate it with gold and put it on a chain and wear it around your neck."

"I want you to use it."

Then I started thinking maybe this guy was some kind of a sadist. A caliber of .50 is a decimal fraction, just another way of saying half an inch. A lead bullet a half inch across is a big thing. It weighs about two ounces, and any kind of a decent load fires it close to two thousand miles an hour. It could catch a supersonic jet fighter and bring it down. Against a person two hundred yards away, it's going to cut him in two. Like making the guy swallow a bomb, and then setting it off.

I said, "You want a spectacle, I could do it close with a knife. You know, if you want to send a message."

He said, "That's not the issue. This is not about a message. This is about the result."

"Can't be," I said. "From two hundred yards I can get a result with anything. Something short with a folding stock,

I can walk away afterward with it under my coat. Or I could throw a rock."

"I want you to use the Barrett."

"Expensive," I said. "I'd have to leave it behind. Which means paying through the nose to make it untraceable. It'll cost more than a foreign car for the ordnance alone. Before we even talk about my fee."

"Okay," he said, no hesitation.

I said, "It's ridiculous."

He said nothing. I thought: *Two hundred yards, no body armor, in the open air. Makes no sense.* So I asked.

I said, "Who's the target?"

He said, "A horse."

I was quiet for a long moment. "What kind of a horse?"

"A Thoroughbred racehorse."

I asked, "You own racehorses?"

He said, "Dozens of them."

"Good ones?"

"Some of the very best."

"So the target is what, a rival?"

"A thorn in my side."

After that, it made a lot more sense. The guy said, "I'm not an idiot. I've thought about it very carefully. It's got to look accidental. We can't just shoot the horse in the head. That's too obvious. It's got to look like the real target was the owner, but your aim was off and the horse is collateral damage. So the shot can't look placed. It's got to look random. Neck, shoulder, whatever. But I need death or permanent disability."

I said, "Which explains your preference for the Barrett."

He nodded. I nodded back. A Thoroughbred racehorse weighs about half a ton. A .308 or a NATO round fired randomly into its center mass might not do the job. Not in terms of death or permanent disability. But a big .50 shell almost certainly would. Even if you weigh half a ton, it's pretty hard to struggle along with a hole the size of a garbage can blown through any part of you.

I asked, "Who's the owner? Is he a plausible target in himself?"

The guy told me who the owner was, and we agreed he was a plausible target. Rumors, shady connections.

Then I said, "What about you? Are you two enemies, personally?"

"You mean, will I be suspected of ordering the hit that misses?"

"Exactly."

"Not a chance," my guy said. "We don't know each other."

"Except as rival owners."

"There are hundreds of rival owners."

"Is a horse of yours going to win if this guy's doesn't?"

"I certainly hope so."

"So they'll look at you."

"Not if it looks like the man was the target, instead of the horse."

I asked, "When?"

He told me anytime within the next four days.

I asked, "Where?"

He told me the horse was in a facility some ways south. Horse country, obviously, grand fields, lush grass, white fences, rolling hills. He told me about long routes through the countryside, called gallops, where the horses worked out just after dawn. He told me about the silence and the early mists. He told me how in the week before a big race the owner would be there every morning to assess his horse's form, to revel in its power and speed and grace and appetite. He told me about the stands of trees that were everywhere and would provide excellent cover. Then he stopped talking. I felt a little foolish, but I asked him anyway: "Do you have a photograph? Of the target?"

He took an envelope from his inside jacket pocket. Gave it to me. In it was a glossy color picture of a horse. It looked posed, like a promotional item. Like an actor or an actress has headshots made, for publicity. This particular horse was a magnificent animal. Tall, shiny, muscular, almost jet-black, with a white blaze on its face. Quite beautiful.

"Okay," I said.

Then my guy asked me his own question.

He asked me, "How much?"

It was an interesting issue. Technically we were only conspiring to shoot a horse. In most states that's a property crime. A long way from homicide. And I already had an untraceable Barrett Ninety. As a matter of fact, I had three. Their serial numbers stopped dead with the Israeli army. One of them was well used. It was about ready for a new barrel anyway. It would make a fine throw-down gun. Firing cold through a worn barrel wasn't something I would risk against a human, but against something the size of a horse from two hundred yards it wouldn't be a problem. If I aimed at the fattest part of the animal I could afford to miss by up to a foot.

I didn't tell the guy any of that, of course. Instead I banged on for a while about the price of the rifle and the premium I would have to pay for dead-ended paperwork. Then I talked about risk, and waited to see if he stopped me. But he didn't. I could tell he was obsessed. He had a goal. He wanted his own horse to win, and that fact was blinding him to reality just the same way some people get all wound up about betrayal and adultery and business partnerships.

I looked at the photograph again.

"One hundred thousand dollars," I said.

He said nothing.

"In cash," I said.

He said nothing.

"Up front," I said.

He nodded.

"One condition," he said. "I want to be there. I want to see it happen."

I looked at him and I looked at the photograph and I thought about a hundred grand in cash.

"Okay," I said. "You can be there."

He opened the briefcase he had down by his leg and took out a brick of money. It looked okay, smelled okay, and felt okay. There was probably more in the case, but I didn't care. A hundred grand was enough, in the circumstances.

"Day after tomorrow," I said.

We agreed on a place to meet, down south, down in horse country, and he left.

———

I hid the money where I always do, which is in a metal trunk in my storage unit. Inside the trunk the first thing you see is a human skull inside a Hefty OneZip bag. On the white panel where you're supposed to write what you're freezing is lettered: *This Man Tried to Rip Me Off.* It isn't true, of course. The skull came from an antique shop. Probably an old medical school specimen from the Indian subcontinent.

Next to the money trunk was the gun trunk. I took out the worn Barrett and checked it over. Disassembled it, cleaned it, oiled it, wiped it clean, and then put it back together wearing latex gloves. I loaded a fresh magazine, still with the gloves on. Then I loaded the magazine into the rifle and slid the rifle end-on into an old shoulder-borne golf bag. Then I put the golf bag into the trunk of my car and left it there.

In my house I propped the racehorse photograph on my mantel. I spent a lot of time staring at it.

—

I met the guy at the time and place we had agreed. It was a lonely crossroad, close to a cross-country track that led to a distant stand of trees, an hour before dawn. The weather was cold. My guy had a coat and gloves on, and binoculars around his neck. I had gloves on too. Latex. But no binoculars. I had a Leupold & Stevens scope on the Barrett, in the golf bag.

I was relaxed, feeling what I always feel when I'm about to kill something, which is to say nothing very much at all. But my client was unrelaxed. He was shivering with an anticipation that was almost pornographic in its intensity. Like a pedophile on a plane to Thailand. I didn't like it much.

We walked side by side through the dew. The ground was hard and pocked by footprints. Lots of them, coming and going.

"Who's been here?" I asked.

"Racetrack touts," my guy said. "Sports journalists, gamblers looking for inside dope."

"Looks like Times Square," I said. "I don't like it."

"It'll be okay today. Nobody scouts here anymore. They all know this horse. They all know it can win in its sleep."

We walked on in silence. Reached the stand of trees. It was oval shaped, thin at the northern end. We stepped back and forth until we had a clear line of sight through the trunks. Dawn light was in the sky. Two hundred yards away and slightly downhill was a broad grass clearing with plenty of tire tracks showing. A thin gray mist hung in the air.

"This is it?" I said.

My guy nodded. "The horses come in from the south. The cars come in from the west. They meet right there."

"Why?"

"No real reason. Ritual, mostly. Backslapping and bullshitting. The pride of ownership."

I took the Barrett out of the golf bag. I had already decided how I was going to set up the shot. No bipod. I wanted the gun low and free. I knelt on one knee and rested the muzzle in the crook of a branch. Sighted through the scope. Racked the bolt and felt the first mighty .50 shell smack home into the chamber.

"Now we wait," my guy said. He stood at my shoulder, maybe a yard to my right and a yard behind me.

———

The cars arrived first. They were SUVs, really. Working machines, old and muddy and dented. A Jeep, and two Land Rovers. Five guys climbed out. Four looked poor and one looked rich.

"Trainer and stable boys and the owner," my guy said. "The owner is the one in the long coat."

The five of them stamped and shuffled and their breath pooled around their heads.

"Listen," my guy said.

I heard something way off to my left. To the south. A low drumming, and a sound like giant bellows coughing and pumping. Hooves, and huge equine lungs cycling gallons of sweet fresh morning air.

I rocked backward until I was sitting right down on the ground.

"Get ready," my guy said, from above and behind me.

There were altogether ten horses. They came up in a ragged arrowhead formation, slowing, drifting off-line, tossing their heads, their hard breathing blowing violent yard-long trumpet-shaped plumes of steam ahead of them.

"What is this?" I asked. "The whole roster?"

"String," my guy said. "That's what we call it. This is his whole first string."

In the gray dawn light and under the steam all the horses looked exactly the same to me.

But that didn't matter.

"Ready?" my guy said. "They won't be here long."

"Open your mouth," I said.

"What?"

"Open your mouth, real wide. Like you're yawning."

"Why?"

"To equalize the pressure. Like on a plane. I told you, this is a loud gun. It's going to blow your eardrums otherwise. You'll be deaf for a month."

I glanced around and checked. He had opened his mouth, but half-heartedly, like a guy waiting for the dentist to get back from looking at a chart.

"No, like this," I said. I showed him. I opened my mouth as wide as it would go and pulled my chin back into my neck until the tendons hurt in the hinge of my jaw.

He did the same thing.

I whipped the Barrett's barrel way up and around, fast and smooth, like a duck hunter tracking a flushed bird. Then I pulled the trigger. Shot my guy through the roof of his mouth. The giant rifle boomed and kicked and the top of my guy's head came off like a hard-boiled egg. His body came down in a heap and sprawled. I dropped the rifle on top of him and pulled his right shoe off. Tossed it on the ground. Then I ran. Two minutes later I was back in my car. Four minutes later I was a mile away.

———

I was up an easy hundred grand, but the world was down an industrialist, a philanthropist, and a racehorse owner. That's what the Sunday papers said. He had committed suicide. The way the cops had pieced it together, he had tormented himself over the fact that

73

his best horse always came in second. He had spied on his rival's workout, maybe hoping for some sign of fallibility. None had been forthcoming. So he had somehow obtained a sniper rifle, last legally owned by the Israel Defense Force. Maybe he had planned to shoot the rival horse, but at the last minute he hadn't been able to go through with it. So, depressed and tormented, he had reversed the rifle, put the muzzle in his mouth, kicked off his shoe, and used his toe on the trigger. A police officer of roughly the same height had taken part in a simulation to prove that such a thing was physically possible, even with a gun as long as the Barrett.

Near the back of the paper were the racing results. The big black horse had won by seven lengths. My guy's runner had been scratched.

I kept the photograph on my mantel for a long time afterward. A girl I met much later noticed that it was the only picture I had in the house. She asked me if I liked animals better than people. I told her that I did, mostly. She liked me for it. But not enough to stick around.

# PUBLIC TRANSPORTATION

He said he wouldn't talk to me. I asked him why. He said because he was a cop and I was a journalist. I said he sounded like a guy with something to hide. He said no, he had nothing to hide.

"So talk to me," I said, and I knew he would.

He scuffed around for a minute more, hands on the top of the bar, drumming his fingers, moving a little on his stool. I knew him fairly well. He was edging out of the summer of his career and entering the autumn. His best years were behind him. He was in the valley, facing a long ten years before his pension. He liked winning, but losing didn't worry him too much. He was a realistic man. But he liked to be sure. What he hated was not really knowing whether he had won or lost.

"From the top," I said.

He shrugged and took a sip of his beer and sighed and blew fumes toward the mirror facing us. Then he started with the 911 call. The house, out beyond Chandler, south and east of the city. A long low ranch, prosperous, walled in, the unlit pool, the darkness. The parents, arriving home from a party. The silence. The busted window, the empty bed. The trail of blood through the hallway. The daughter's body, all ripped up. Fourteen years old, damaged in a way he still wasn't prepared to discuss.

I said, "There were details that you withheld."

He asked, "How do you know?"

"You guys always do that. To evaluate the confessions."

He nodded.

I asked, "How many confessions did you get?"

"A hundred and eight."

"All phony?"

"Of course."

"What information did you withhold?"

"I'm not going to tell you."

"Why not? You not sure you got the right guy?"

He didn't answer.

"Keep going," I said.

So he did. The scene was clearly fresh. The parents had gotten back maybe moments after the perpetrator had exited. Police response had been fast. The blood on the hallway carpet was still liquid. Dark red, not black, against the kid's pale skin. The kid's pale skin was a problem from the start. They all knew it. They were in a position to act fast and heavy, so they were going to, and they

knew it would be claimed later that the speed was all about the kid
being white, not black or brown. It wasn't. It was a question of luck
and timing. They got a fresh scene, and they got a couple of breaks.
I nodded, like I accepted his view. Which I did. I was a journalist,
and I liked mischief as much as the next guy, but sometimes things
were straightforward.

"Go on," I said.

There were photographs of the kid all over the house. She was
an only child. She was luminous and beautiful. She was stupefying,
the way fourteen-year-old white Arizona girls often are.

"Go on," I said.

The first break had been the weather. There had been torrential
rain two days previously, and then the heat had come back with
a vengeance. The rain had skimmed the street with sand and
mud and the heat had baked it to a film of dust, and the dust
showed no tire tracks other than those from the parents' vehicle
and the cop cars and the ambulance. Therefore the perpetrator
had arrived on foot. And left on foot. There were clear marks in
the dust. Sneakers, maybe size ten, fairly generic soles. The prints
were photographed and e-mailed and everyone was confident that
in the fullness of time some database somewhere would match
a brand and a style. But what was more important was that they
had a suspect recently departed from a live scene on foot, in a
landscape where no one walked. So APBs and be-on-the-lookouts
were broadcast for a two-mile radius. It was midnight and more
than a hundred degrees and pedestrians were going to be rare. It
was simply too hot for walking. Certainly too hot for running.
Any kind of sustained physical activity would be close to a suicide

attempt. Greater Phoenix was that kind of place, especially in the summer.

Ten minutes passed and no fugitives were found.

Then they got their second break. The parents were reasonably lucid. In between all the bawling and screaming they noticed their daughter's cell phone was missing. It had been her pride and joy. An Apple iPhone, with an AT&T contract that gave her unlimited minutes, which she exploited to the max. Back then iPhones were new and cool. The cops figured the perp had stolen it. They figured the kind of guy who had no car in Arizona would have been entranced by a small shiny object like an iPhone. Or else if he was some kind of big-time deviant, maybe he collected souvenirs. Maybe the cache of photographs of the kid's friends was exciting. Or the text messages stored in the memory.

"Go on," I said.

The third break was all about middle-class parents and fourteen-year-old daughters. The parents had signed up for a service whereby they could track the GPS chip in the iPhone on their home computer. Not cheap, but they were the kind of people that wanted to know their kid was telling the truth when she said she was sleeping over at a girlfriend's house or riding with a buddy to the library. The cops got the password and logged on right there and then and saw the phone moving slowly north, toward Tempe. Too fast for walking. Too fast for running. Too slow to be in a car.

"Bike?" one of them said.

"Too hot," another answered. "Plus no tire tracks in the driveway."

The guy telling the story next to me on his stool had been the one who had understood.

"Bus," he said. "The perp is on the bus."

Greater Phoenix had a lot of buses. They were for workers paid too little to own cars. They shuttled folks around, especially early in the morning and late at night. The giant city would have ground to a halt without them. Meals would have gone unserved, pools uncleaned, beds unmade, trash not collected. Immediately all the cops as one imagined a rough profile. A dark-skinned man, probably small, probably crazy, rocking on a seat as a bus headed north. Fiddling with the iPhone, checking the music library, looking at the pictures. Maybe with the knife still in his pocket, although surely that was too much to ask.

One cop stayed at the house and watched the screen and called the game like a sports announcer. All the APBs and the BOLOs were canceled and every car screamed after the bus. It took ten minutes to find it. Ten seconds to stop it. It was corralled in a ring of cars. Lights were flashing and popping and cops were crouching behind hoods and doors and trunks and guns were pointing, Glocks and shotguns, dozens of them.

The bus had a driver and three passengers aboard.

The driver was a woman. All three passengers were women. All three were elderly. One of them was white. The driver was a skinny Hispanic of thirty.

"Go on," I said.

The guy beside me sipped his beer again and sighed. He had arrived at the point where the investigation was botched. They had spent close to twenty minutes questioning the four women, searching them, making them move up and down the street while the cop back at the house watched for GPS action on the screen. But the cursor didn't move. The phone was still on the bus. But the bus was empty. They searched under the seats. Nothing. They searched the seats themselves.

They found the phone.

The last-but-one seat at the back on the right had been slit with a knife. The phone had been forced edgewise into the foam rubber cushion. It was hidden there and bleeping away silently. A wild goose chase. A decoy.

The slit in the seat was rimed with faint traces of blood. The same knife.

The driver and all three passengers recalled a white man getting on the bus south of Chandler. He had seated himself in back and gotten out again at the next stop. He was described as neatly dressed and close to middle age. He was remembered for being from the wrong demographic. Not a typical bus rider.

The cops asked, "Was he wearing sneakers?"

No one knew for sure.

"Did he have blood on him?"

No one recalled.

The chase restarted south of Chandler. The assumption was that because the decoy had been placed to move north, then the perp was actually moving south. A fine theory, but it came to nothing. No one was found. A helicopter joined the effort. The night was still dark but the helicopter had thermal imaging equipment. It was not useful. Everything single thing it saw was hot.

Dawn came and the helicopter refueled and came back for a visual search. And again, and again, for days. At the end of a long weekend it found something.

"Go on," I said.

The thing that the helicopter found was a corpse. White male, wearing sneakers. In his early twenties. He was identified as a college student, last seen the day before. A day later the medical examiner issued his report. The guy had died of heat exhaustion and dehydration.

"Consistent with running from a crime scene?" the cops asked.

"Among other possibilities," the medical examiner answered.

The guy's toxicology screen was baroque. Ecstasy, skunk, alcohol.

"Enough to make him unstable?" the cops asked.

"Enough to make an elephant unstable," the medical examiner answered.

The guy beside me finished his beer. I signaled for another.

I asked, "Case closed?"

The guy beside me nodded. "Because the kid was white. We needed a result."

"You not convinced?"

"He wasn't middle aged. He wasn't neatly dressed. His sneakers were wrong. No sign of the knife. Plus a guy hopped-up enough to run himself to death in the heat wouldn't have thought to set up the decoy with the phone."

"So who was he?"

"Just a frat boy who liked partying a little too much."

"Anyone share your opinion?"

"All of us."

"Anyone doing anything about it?"

"The case is closed."

"So what really happened?"

"I think the decoy indicates premeditation. And I think it was a double bluff. I think the perp got out of the bus and carried on north, maybe in a car he had parked."

I nodded. The perp had. Right then the car he had used was parked in the lot behind the bar. Its keys were in my pocket.

"Win some, lose some," I said.

# ME & MR. RAFFERTY

I can tell what kind of night it was by where I wake up. If I've been good, I'm in bed. If I've been bad, I'm on the sofa. Good or bad, you understand, only in the conventional sense of the words. The moral sense. The legal sense. I'm always good in terms of performance. Always careful, always meticulous, always unbeatable. Let's be clear about that. But let's just say that some specific nighttime activities stress me more than others, tire me, waste me, leave me vulnerable to sudden collapse as soon as I step back into the sanctuary behind my own front door.

This morning I wake up on the hallway floor.

My face is pressed down on the carpet. I can taste its fibers on my lips. I need a cigarette. I open one eye, slowly, and move my eyeball, slowly, left and right, up and down, looking for what I need. But before we go on, let's be clear: However haltingly you read these words, however generously you interpret the word *slowly*, however deep and 16-RPM and *s-l-o-w* your voice, however much you try to get into it, you are certain to be racing, to be galloping insanely fast, to be moving close to the fucking *speed of light*, compared to what is actually happening in terms of my ocular deployment. The part with the eyelid alone must have taken close to five minutes. The eyeball rotation, four points of the compass, at least five minutes each.

A bad night.

I am pretty sure I have a fresh pack of cigarettes on the low table in the living room. I concentrate hard in that direction. I see them. I am disappointed. Not a fresh pack. An almost-fresh pack. A pack, in fact, in the condition I like least: recently unwrapped, the crisp little cardboard lid raised up, and one cigarette missing from the front row. I hate that for two reasons: First, the pack looks violated. Like a dear, dear friend with a front tooth punched out. Ugly. And second, however hard I try to prevent it, the sight sends me spiraling back to grade-school arithmetic: There are twenty cigarettes in a new pack, arranged in three rows, and twenty is *not fucking divisible by three.* I see a pack like that and instantly I am full of rage and paranoia: The tobacco companies are lying to me. Which, of course, they would. They have an accomplished track record in that department. For forty years I have been paying for twenty, and all along they have been supplying me with eighteen. Eighteen is divisible by three. As is twenty-one, but are you seriously suggesting the tobacco companies would supply *more* than a person pays for?

So I lie and pant, but again, let's be clear: The oldest, tiredest dog you ever saw sighs a hundred million times faster than I was panting. We're talking glacial inhalations and exhalations. Whole species could spark and evolve and go extinct between each of my morning breaths.

I had left cigarette butts at the scene. Two of them, Camels, close to but not actually mired in the spreading pool of blood. Deliberately, of course. I know exactly how the game is played. I'm not new to this. The police need the illusion of progress. Not *actual* progress, necessarily, but they need something to tell reporters, they need smug smiles and video of important things being carried away in small opaque evidence bags. So I play along. It's in my interests to give them what they need. I give Mr. Rafferty things to smile about, and I'm absolutely sure he knows they're gifts.

But they're useless. A cigarette smoked carefully in dry air retains almost no saliva. No DNA. No fingerprints, either. The paper is wrong, and most of it burns anyway, at a temperature close to two thousand degrees. So the gifts cost me nothing, and they give me the satisfaction of knowing I am playing my part in keeping the whole show on the road.

I move the fingers of my right hand and make a claw and start to scrabble microscopically against the resistance of the rug. I have future events to plan: getting to my knees, standing upright, stripping, showering, dressing again. A long agenda, and many hours of work. No breakfast, of course. Long ago I decided that respect for minimum standards of propriety forbade eating after killing. I am hungry, make no mistake, but the promised cigarette will help with that. Plus coffee. I will make a pot and drink it all and compare its thin fluidity to blood. Blood is less viscous than people think, especially when generated in the kind of volume that my work produces. It splashes and spatters and runs and drains. It is spectacular, which is the point: Obviously Mr. Rafferty does not want to work cases that are mundane, or trivial, or merely sordid. Mr. Rafferty wants a large canvas, and a large canvas is what I give him.

I push with my left palm and ease my shoulders an inch off the floor. The pressure is relieved from my cheek. I am sure the flesh will be red and stippled there. I am not young. My face is doughy and white. Tone has gone. But I can pass it off as razor burn, or bourbon. I focus again on the almost-fresh pack ten feet from me. Tantalizing, and for now as distant as the moon. But I will get there. Trust me.

I have no clear recollection of last night's events. The details are for Mr. Rafferty to discover. I sow, he reaps. It is a partnership. But lest you misunderstand: My victims deserve to die. I am not a monster. I have many inflexible rules. I target only certain kinds of repulsive criminals; I never hurt women or children. I look for the people Mr. Rafferty can't reach. And not hapless, low-level street pimps or escort bookers, either: I set my sights a little higher. Not too high, though: for that way lies frustration. Neither Mr. Rafferty nor I can get to the real movers and shakers. But there is a wide layer of smug, culpable people between the two extremes. That is where I hunt. For two reasons: I can feel a glow of public service, and, more importantly, such careful selection puts Mr. Rafferty in a most delicious bind. He wins by losing. He loses by winning. The longer he fails to find me, the more the city is relieved of bad people. The reporters he deals with understand, although they don't say so out loud. Everyone—me, Mr. Rafferty, citizens, inhabitants—benefits from perfect equilibrium.

Long may it continue.

Now I have to decide whether to roll right or left. It has to be one or the other. It's the only way I can get up off the floor. I am not young. I am no longer agile. I decide to roll left. I stretch my left arm high so that my shoulder goes small and I push with my right. I roll onto my back. A significant victory. Now I am well on the way to rising. I know that Mr. Rafferty is getting up, too, ready to start his day. Soon he will get the call: another one! Hung upside down, as I recall, zip-tied to a chain-link fence that surrounds a long-abandoned construction zone, gagged, abused, eventually nicked in a hundred places, veins, arteries, throat. I don't recall specifically, but I imagine I finished with the femoral artery, where it runs close to the surface in the groin. It's a wide vessel, and, given adequate pressure from a thumping heart, it spurts high in a wonderful ruby arc. I imagine the man jerked his chin to his chest to look up in horror; I imagine I asked him how he was enjoying his BMW *now, asshole,* and his big house and his Caribbean vacations and his freebies with the poor Romanian girls he imports with all kinds of false promises about jobs with Saks Fifth Avenue before turning them loose to perform disgusting acts for six hundred dollars an hour, most of which he keeps, until the girls grow too addicted and haggard to earn anything anymore.

Not that I care about either Romania or the girls. I have no enthusiasm for any part of Eastern Europe, and prostitution has always been with us. Although I know the man I tied to the fence also runs Brazilian girls, and I care for them to some slight extent. Sweet, dark, shy creatures. I partake regularly, in fact, in that arena, which is what led me to the man himself. A girl I rented, less than half my age, recited on request the menu of services she offered, some of which were truly exotic, and I asked her if she really liked doing those things. Like all good whores she faked great enthusiasm at first, but I was relentlessly skeptical: You *enjoy* sticking your tongue deep into a stranger's anus? Eventually she confessed she was obliged to, at risk of getting beaten. At that moment the man's fate was sealed, and I imagine I used a stick before I used the knife. I care about justice, you see, and the whole what-goes-around-comes-around thing.

But mostly I care about the equilibrium, and the partnership, and keeping Mr. Rafferty in work. He is a veteran homicide cop, my age exactly, and I like to think we understand each other, and that he needs me.

It is time to sit up. And because written narrative has its conventions, let me again be clear: A long time has passed. My thoughts, however presented on the page, have been halting and disconnected and have taken a long time to form. We are not talking about a burst of decisive energy here. This process is slow. I walk my hands back above my waist, I raise my head, I twist and lever, I sit up.

Then I rest.

And I confess: It is about more than just equilibrium and partnership. It is about the contest. Me and Mr. Rafferty. Him against me. Who will win? Perhaps neither of us, ever. We seem to be perfectly matched. Perhaps equilibrium is a result, not a goal.

Perhaps we both enjoy the journey, and perhaps we both fear the destination.

Perhaps we can make this last forever.

I scan ahead through my morning tasks. The ultimate objective, as for so many, is to get to work on time. My day job, I suppose I should call it. Punctuality is expected. So less than an hour after sitting up I gather my feet under me and rise, hands out to steady myself against the walls, two staggering steps to establish balance, a lurch in the general direction of the living room, and the prize is mine: my morning smoke. I pull a second cigarette from the pack and close the lid so as not to see two busted teeth; gaze around, trusting in the eternal truth that wherever cigarettes may be, there will be a lighter close by. I find a yellow Bic a yard away and thumb its tiny wheel; I light the smoke and inhale deeply, gratefully, and then I cough and blink, and the day finally accelerates.

The shower is soothing: I use disinfectant soap, a carbolic product similar to medical issue. Not that I carry trace evidence; I am not new to this game. But I like cleanliness. I check myself in the mirror very carefully. The carpet burn on my cheek is noticeable, but generalized, like a normal Irish flush; it is entirely appropriate. I part my hair and comb it flat. I unwrap a shirt and put it on. I select a suit: It is not new and not clean, made from a heavy gabardine that smells faintly of sweat and smoke and the thousand other odors a city dweller absorbs. I tie my tie, I slip on my shoes, I collect the items a man in my position carries.

I head outside. My employer provides a car; I start it up and drive. It is still early. Traffic is light. There is nothing untoward on the radio. The abandoned construction zone is as yet unvisited by dog walkers.

I arrive. I park. I head inside. Like everywhere, my place of employment has a receptionist. Not a model-pretty young woman like some places I have seen; instead, a burly man in a sergeant's uniform.

He says, "Good morning, Mr. Rafferty."

I return his greeting and head onward, to the squad room.

# SECTION 7 (A) (OPERATIONAL)

T he team first came together late one Tuesday evening in my apartment. There was none of the usual gradualism about the process; I had none of them, and then I had all of them. Their sudden appearance as a complete unit was certainly gratifying, but also unexpected, and therefore I was less immediately grateful than perhaps I could have been, or should have been, because I was immediately on guard for negative implications. Was I being rolled? Had they come with an established agenda? I had begun the process days before, in the normal way, which was to make tentative approaches to the key players, or at least to let it be known that I was in the market for certain *types* of key players, and normally the process would have continued over a number of weeks, in an accretional way, a commitment secured here, a second commitment there, with an accompanying daisy chain of personal recommendations and suggestions, followed by patient recruitment of specialist operators, until all was finally in place.

But they all came at once. I was reluctant to let myself believe such an event was a response to my reputation; after all, my reputation has neither increased nor decreased in value for many years, and I never met a response like that before. Nor, I felt, could it be a response to my years of experience; the truth was I had long ago transitioned to the status of an old hand, and generally I felt my appeal had been dulled by over-familiarity. Which was why I looked the gift horse in the mouth: as I said, I was suspicious.

But I observed that they seemed not to know one another, which was reassuring, and which removed my fears of a prior conspiracy against me, and they were certainly appropriately attentive to me: I got no feeling that I was to be a passenger on my own ship. But I remained suspicious nonetheless, which slowed things down; and I think I might even have offended them a little, with my slightly tepid response. But: Better safe than sorry, which I felt was a sentiment I could rely on them to understand.

My living room is not small—it was two rooms before I removed a wall—but even so, it was somewhat crowded. I was on the sofa that gets the view, smoking, and they were facing me in a rough semicircle, three of them shoulder to shoulder on the sofa that faces mine, and the others on furniture brought in from other rooms, except for two men I had never met before, who stood side by side close behind the others. They were both tall and solid and dark, and they were both looking at me with poor-bloody-infantry expressions on their faces, partly resigned and stoic, and partly appealing, as if they were pleading with me not to get them killed too soon. They were clearly foot soldiers—which, obviously, I needed—but they weren't the hapless, runty, conscripted kind: indeed, how could they be? They had volunteered, like everyone else. And they were fine physical specimens, no doubt trained and deadly in all the ways I would need them to be. They wore suit coats, of excellent quality in terms of cut and cloth, but rubbed and greasy where they were tight over ledges of hard muscle.

There were two women. They had dragged the counter stools in from the kitchen, and they were perched on them, behind and to the right of the three men on the sofa—a kind of mezzanine seating arrangement. I admit I was disappointed that there were only two of them: A mix of two women and eight men was borderline unacceptable by the current standards of our trade, and I was reluctant to open myself to criticism that could have been avoided at the start. Not public criticism, of course—the public was generally almost completely unaware of what we did—but insider criticism, from the kind of professional gatekeepers who could influence future assignments.

And I wasn't impressed by the way the women had positioned themselves slightly behind the men: I felt it spoke of the kind of subservience I would normally seek to avoid. They were very nice to look at, though, which delighted me at the time, but only reinforced my anticipation of later carping. Both wore skirts, neither one excessively short, but their perching on high stools showed me more thigh than I felt they intended. They were both wearing dark nylons, which I readily admit is my favorite mode of dress for shapely legs, and I was truly distracted for a moment. But then I persuaded myself—on a provisional basis only, always subject to confirmation—that they were serious professionals, and would indeed be seen as such, and so for the time being I let my worries go, and I moved on.

The man on the right of the group had brought in the Eames lounge chair from the foyer, but not the ottoman. He was sitting in the chair, leaning back in its contour with his legs crossed at the knee, and he made an elegant impression. He was wearing a gray suit. I assumed from the start that he was my government liaison man, and I was proved right. I had worked with many similar men, and I felt I could take his habits and abilities on trust. Mistakes are made that way, of course, but I was confident I wasn't making one that night. The only thing that unsettled me was that he had positioned his chair an inch farther away from the main group than was strictly necessary. As I said, my living room is not small, but neither is it infinitely spacious: That extra inch had been hard won. Clearly it spoke of a need or an attitude, and I was aware from the start that I should pay attention to it.

My dining chairs are the Tulip design by the Finnish designer Eero Saarinen; both now flanked the sofa opposite me and were occupied by men I assumed were my transport coordinator and my communications expert. Initially I paid little attention to the men, because the chairs themselves had put me in a minor fugue: Saarinen had, of course, also designed the TWA Flight Center at John F. Kennedy Airport—or Idlewild, as it was called at the time—which building had quite rightly become an icon, and an absolute symbol of its era. It recalled the days when the simple word "jet" meant much more than merely a propulsive engine. Jet

plane, jet set, jet travel . . . the new Boeing 707, impossibly fast and
sleek, the glamour, the larger horizons, the bigger world. In my
trade we all know we are competing with the legends whose best
work—while not necessarily *performed* in—was indisputably *rooted*
in that never-to-be-repeated age. Periodically I feel completely
inadequate to the challenge, and indeed for several minutes that
particular evening I felt like sending everyone away and giving up
before I had even started.

But I reassured myself by reminding myself that the new world
is challenging too, and that those old-timers might well run
screaming if faced with the kind of things we have to deal with
now—like male-to-female ratios, for instance, and their mutual
interactions. So I stopped looking at the chairs and started looking
at the men, and I found nothing to worry about. Frankly, transport
is an easy job—merely a matter of budget, and I had no practical
constraint on what I was about to spend. Communications get
more complex every year, but generally a conscientious engineer can
handle what is thrown at him. The popular myth that computers
can be operated only by pierced youths whose keyboards are buried
under old pizza boxes and skateboards is nonsense, of course. I have
always used exactly what had arrived: a serious technician with a
measured and cautious manner.

On my left on the sofa opposite me was what I took to be our
mole. I was both pleased with and worried by him. Pleased, in
the sense that it was obvious he had been born in-country, almost
certainly in Tehran or one of its closer suburbs. That was indisput-
able. His DNA was absolutely correct; I was sure it was absolutely
authentic. It was what lay over his DNA that worried me. I was

sure that when I investigated further I would find he had left Iran at a young age and come to America. Which generally makes for the best moles: unquestioned ethnic authenticity, and unquestioned loyalty to our side. But—and perhaps I am more sensitive to this issue than my colleagues—those formative years in America leave physical traces as well as mental. The vitamin-enriched cereals, the milk, the cheeseburgers—they make a difference. If, for instance, due to some bizarre circumstance, this young man had a twin brother who had been left behind, and I now compared them side by side, I had no doubt our mole would be at least an inch taller and five pounds heavier than his sibling. No big deal, you might say, in the vernacular, and I might agree—except that the *kind* of inch and the *kind* of pound does matter. A big, self-confident, straight-backed *American* inch matters a great deal. Five *American* pounds—in the chest and the shoulders, not the gut—matter enormously. Whether I had time to make him lose the weight and correct the posture remained to be seen. If not, in my opinion, we would be going into action with a major source of uncertainty at the very heart of our operation. But then, when in our business have we ever not?

At the other end of the sofa opposite me was our traitor. He was a little older than middle-aged, unshaven, a little fat, a little gray, dressed in a rumpled suit that was clearly the product of foreign tailoring. His shirt was creased and buttoned at the neck and worn without a tie. Like all traitors he would be motivated by either ideology, or money, or blackmail. I hoped it would prove to be money. I'm suspicious of ideology. Of course it gives me a warm feeling when a man risks everything because he thinks my country is better than his; but such a conviction carries with it the smack of fanaticism, and fanaticism is inherently unstable, even readily changeable: In the white heat of a fanatic's mind, even an imagined slight of the most trivial kind can produce mulish results. Blackmail is inherently changeable too: What is an embarrassment one day might not always be. Think back to those jet-set days: homosexuality and honey-trap infidelities produced riches beyond measure. Would we get a tenth of the response today? I think not. But money always works. Money is addictive. Recipients get a taste for it, and they can't quit. Our boy's inside information would clearly be absolutely crucial, so I hoped he was bought and paid for, otherwise we would be adding a second layer of uncertainty into the mix. Not, as I said, that there isn't always uncertainty at the heart of what we do: But too much is too much. It's as simple as that.

Between the mole and the traitor was the man clearly destined to lead the operation. He was what I think we would all want in that position. Privately I believe that a cross-referenced graph of the rise and fall of mental versus physical capabilities in men would show a clear composite peak around the age of thirty-five. Previously—when I have had a choice, that is—I have worked with men not younger than that and not older than forty. I estimated that the man facing me fell neatly in that range. He was compact, neither light nor heavy, and clearly comfortable in his mind and body, and clearly comfortable with his range of competencies. Like a Major League second baseman, perhaps. He knew what he was doing, and he could keep on doing it all day, if he had to. He was not handsome, but not ugly either; again, the athletic comparison was, I felt, apt.

He said, "I'm guessing this is my show."

I said, "You're wrong. It's mine."

I wasn't sure exactly how to characterize the way he had spoken: Was he a humble man pretending not to be? Or was he an arrogant man pretending to be humble pretending not to be? Obviously it was a question I needed to settle, so I didn't speak again. I just waited for his response.

It came in the form of an initial physical gesture: He patted the air in front of him, right-handed, his wrist bent and his palm toward me. It was a motion clearly intended to calm me, but it was also a gesture of submission, rooted in ancient habits: He was showing me he wasn't armed.

"Of course," he said.

I mirrored his gesture: I patted the air, wrist bent, palm open. I felt the repetition extended the meaning; I intended the gesture to say, OK, no harm, no foul, let's replay the point. It interested me that I was again unconsciously thinking in terms of sports metaphors. But this was a team, after all.

I said out loud, "You're the leader *in the field*. You're my eyes and ears. You have to be, really. I can't know what you don't know. But let's be clear. No independent action. You might be the eyes and the ears, but I'm the brain."

I probably sounded too defensive, and unnecessarily so: Casting modesty aside, as one must from time to time, I was, after all, reasonably well known among a narrow slice of interested parties for my many successful operations in charge of a notably headstrong individual. I was competent in my role, no question. I should have trusted myself a little more. But it was late, and I was tired.

The government liaison man rescued me. He said, "We need to talk about exactly what it is we're going to do."

Which surprised me for a moment: Why had I assembled a team before the mission was defined? But he was right: Beyond the fact that we would be going to Iran—and let's face it, today all of us go to Iran—no details had yet been settled.

The traitor said, "It has to be about nuclear capability."

One of the women said, "Of course—what else is there, really?"

I noted that she had a charming voice. Warm, and a little intimate. In the back of my mind I wondered if I could use her in a seduction role. Or would that get me in even more trouble, with the powers that be?

The communications man said, "There's the issue of regional influence. Isn't that important? But hey, what do I know?"

The government man said, "Their regional influence depends entirely on their nuclear threat."

I let them talk like that for a spell. I was happy to listen and observe. I saw that the two bruisers at the back were getting bored. They had above-my-pay-grade looks on their faces. One of them asked me, "Can we go? You know the kind of thing we can do. You can give us the details later. Would that be OK?"

I nodded. It was fine with me. One of them looked back from the door with his earlier expression: Don't get us killed too soon.

The poor bloody infantry. Silently I promised him not to. I liked him. The others were still deep in discussion. They were twisting and turning and addressing this point and that. The way the Eames chair was so low to the ground, it put the government man's face right next to the right-hand woman's legs. I envied him. But he wasn't impressed. He was more interested in filtering everything that was said through the narrow lens of his own concerns. At one point he looked up at me and asked me directly: "How much State Department trouble do you want exactly?"

Which wasn't as dumb a question as it sounded. It was an eternal truth that very little of substance could be achieved without upsetting the State Department to some degree. And we worked with liaison men for that very reason: They quelled the storm long enough to let us conclude whatever operation was then in play. I thought his question implied an offer: He would do what it took. Which I thought was both generous and brave.

I said, "Look, all of you. Obviously I'll try to make the whole thing as smooth and trouble-free as possible. But we're all grown-ups. We know how it goes. I'll ask for the extra mile if I have to."

Whereupon the transport coordinator asked a related but more mundane question: "How long are we signing up for?"

"Eighty days," I said. "Ninety, maximum. But you know how it is. We won't be in play every day. I want you all to map out a six-month window. I think that's realistic."

Which statement quieted things down a little. But in the end they all nodded and agreed. Which, again, I thought was brave. To use another sports metaphor, they knew the rules of the game. An operation that lasted six months, overseas in hostile territory, was certain to produce casualties. I knew that, and they knew that. Some of them wouldn't be coming home. But none of them flinched.

There was another hour or so of talk, and then another. I felt I got to know them all as well as I needed to. They didn't leave until well into the morning. I called my editor as soon as they were through the door. She asked me how I was, which question from an editor really means, "What have you got for me?"

I told her I was back on track with something pretty good, and that a six-month deadline should see it through. She asked what it was, and I told her it was something that had come to me while I was stoned. I used the tone of voice I always use with her. It leaves her unsure whether I am kidding or not. So she asked again. I said I had the characters down, and that the plot would evolve as it went along. Iran, basically. As a private joke I couched the whole thing in the kind of language we might see in the trade reviews, if we got any: I said it wouldn't transcend the genre, but it would be a solid example of its type.

# ADDICTED TO SWEETNESS

The man calling himself Socrates said to the man in shackles, "White powder has always made money."

The shackles were nothing more than regular handcuffs, four pairs, latched separately to the guy's wrists and ankles, with the empty ends locked into an iron loop set in the floor. As a result, the guy was squatting like a fakir in a pool of liquid, half on his ass and half on his feet, with his knees up and his arms pulled down between them. His head was raised, and his hair was wet and plastered to his skull. He was trying to keep the conversation going, obviously.

He said, "Always?"

"Well, okay, not always," Socrates said. "Not during the Stone Age, maybe. Or the Bronze Age or the Iron Age. The Middle Ages, I'm not sure, either. But certainly for the last three hundred years."

The man in the shackles said, "Sugar."

"Yes," Socrates said, pleased with the response. He was Brazilian by nationality, but ethnically he had all kinds of blood in him. Mayan, Aztec, Carib, some Spanish, some Portuguese, and a long strain of West African from slaves on the island of Antigua. He said, "In the West Indies, sugarcane was grown on every square inch of available land. There was insatiable demand from Europe. Huge fortunes were made. Hard work, though, for those involved."

The man in the shackles said, "Slavery."

"Exactly," Socrates said. "Hoeing, planting, weeding, and harvesting was backbreaking. Boiling and crystallizing was skilled. But it was all done by slaves."

The man in the shackles was white and American, so he said, "Sorry."

Socrates said, "Not your fault. In the West Indies, the owners were British."

The room the two men were in was the ground-floor living room of a suburban house, unoccupied as of an hour ago. The residents had been told to take a long walk, and Socrates had overseen the iron bolt being screwed into the floor, and then his men had taken a long walk, too, but not before bringing in five gallons of gasoline in a can. The guy in the shackles was soaked in it. The liquid that had plastered his hair to his skull was gasoline, and the pool he was sitting in was gasoline. Less than a gallon so far, but a little goes a long way.

Socrates said, "The plantation owners had one fieldworker for every two acres, plus skilled labor for after the harvest, plus domestic staff. As a result, they were heavily outnumbered, twenty to one at times, and they were mistreating their people very badly, working them too hard in the sun, and abusing them in their houses. Especially the females. They had their way with the pretty ones and worked the ugly ones relentlessly."

The man in the shackles said, "Uprisings."

"Yes," Socrates said. "They lived in a permanent state of fear. Quite rightly, I might add. They deserved to. They were always listening out for plots against them. Which were few and far between actually, but they happened."

The man in the shackles didn't speak. Socrates was walking slow circles around the gasoline pool, clockwise, declaiming, enjoying himself, like he imagined his ancient namesake had in the marketplaces of old Athens. He said, "What do you suppose they did when they discovered a planned move against them?"

The man in the shackles said, "Examples."

"Exactly," Socrates said. "They made examples of the ringleaders. They had two favorite methods. Do you know what they were?"

"No."

"The first was breaking on the wheel. Do you know what that was?"

The man in the shackles did know, but he wanted to keep the conversation going, obviously, so he said, "No."

Socrates said, "A man would be stood upright and tied by his wrists and his ankles to a large wagon wheel. Then a fellow slave would be made to break all his bones with a heavy iron bar. All of them, but slowly and in sequence. Possibly an arm first, and then the opposite leg, and so on. The victim would be reduced to a bag of jelly, just hanging there with no effective skeletal support. The agony must have been terrible."

The man in the shackles said, "Yes."

Socrates said, "The second method was to burn them alive. They would be tied to a stake, and a bonfire would be built around them."

The man in the shackles said nothing.

"The power of example," Socrates said. "Very effective. There was trouble, but surprisingly little of it, given that for a long time an overwhelming majority was suffering hideous torment."

The man in the shackles said, "Bad."

Socrates smiled. "But there were enormous profits to safeguard. Then as now. White powder and insatiable demand. Incalculable wealth, something that had never been seen before. Should I burn you alive?"

The man in the shackles said, "No."

"But you stole from me."

"No."

"Half a million dollars is missing."

"Mistake."

"Sloppy bookkeeping?"

"Yes."

"Crystallizing the sugar was an art. The cane was crushed in the mills, and the juice was drained and boiled, and the molasses was skimmed off, and the resulting pure liquid was dried in the sun, and lime was added, and the powder just appeared. That is, if everything was done right. If it wasn't, then money was lost, and the skilled man was beaten severely, often flogged, even though he was a skilled worker and even though the process was difficult and his mistake might have been entirely innocent. Sometimes the victim had a limb cut off, usually a leg. Sometimes he was castrated."

The man in the shackles said nothing.

Socrates said, "It was about the power of example."

The man in the shackles shifted his weight and said, "Pocket change."

"Whose?" Socrates asked, interested. "The plantation owners' or mine?"

"Either one."

"True," Socrates said. "One hogshead of sugar didn't amount to much. A tiny percentage really. Almost invisible, just like a bag of cash is to me."

"Well, then."

"But the big owners had hundreds of slaves. Suppose they all slacked off, just a tiny percentage each? A hogshead here, a hogshead there, weeds in the fields, crops planted too late to get the rain? Then what?"

The man in the shackles didn't answer.

Socrates said, "I have more than hundreds of associates. I have thousands ultimately. Suppose they all made small mistakes?"

"Can't help it. I try hard."

"I'm sure you do. But what if all of you were as sloppy?"

"It was a small amount."

"As was a single hogshead of sugar."

"That's my point. And it was a genuine mistake."

"So you want me to show mercy?"

"Please."

"But then what about the power of example?"

"It was a mistake. That's all."

Socrates stepped over to the corner of the room and picked up the gas can. It was made of red metal, and it had an angled spout. The liquid inside sloshed and moved and exhaled vapor and made thin keening sounds as tiny waves broke against the inside walls. Socrates hefted it high and stepped back to the shackled man and tipped it like a teapot and drizzled a thin stream over the man's head. The man moved, and the stream bathed the hollows above his collarbones and his neck and his back. The man gasped, like the gas was very cold or like he was very afraid or both. Socrates kept it going a full thirty seconds, the best part of another gallon. Then he returned the can to the corner of the room and started walking circles again.

He said, "It was my money, not yours."

The man in the shackles said, "I apologize."

"For what?"

"For the mistake."

"Do you think an apology is enough?"

"Yes."

"Convince me."

The man in the shackles took a deep breath, fully aware that what came next would be crucial. He said, "Any process has inefficiencies at the edges. With the sugar, you know, some of it must have gotten spilled. Some of the liquid must have leaked. It's inevitable. You can't drive yourself crazy, looking for perfection."

"Now you're worried about my spiritual welfare?"

"I'm just saying. There are going to be losses. And mistakes. You can't worry about all of them."

"I don't," Socrates said. "Not all of them. Because you're right. One hundred percent perfection is impossible. Therefore, I set realistic targets."

"Then we're okay."

"No," Socrates said. "We're not okay. Because you exceeded the target. Three hundred grand, maybe four, that's within the margin. But you took five. That's outside the margin."

"But you've got billions. You're a very rich man."

"Actually, I'm an unbelievably rich man."

"So a mistake about half a million is like losing a dime under the sofa cushion."

Socrates took a pack of cigarettes from his pocket, took a cigarette from the pack, and put it between his lips. He held his lighter in his hand. It was a plastic Bic, shaped like a cylinder, disposable, nothing fancy. He didn't spark it up. He just played with it, rotating it fast between his fingers, like a tiny twirling baton. He said, "One assumes that physiologically sugar is important to the human organism in small quantities, but that those small quantities were extremely hard to find in nature so that the craving had to be correspondingly huge and permanent. That's what those old British plantation owners found, anyway. They sold all the sugar they could produce. Demand didn't fall away, even after people were getting enough. They became addicted to sweetness."

The man in the shackles smiled, trying to be a pal. He said, "People are addicted to what we sell, too."

Socrates said, "No, they're addicted to what I sell. There is no 'we' anymore. An hour from now, you won't even be a memory."

The man in the shackles didn't reply. Socrates said, "My point is that those old primeval nutritional urges seem to have hardwired us for addiction. For a million years, we were compelled to seek things out, and we can't stop now. We can't just flip a switch after all of evolutionary history."

"But that's good for us. For our business, I mean."

"Generally," Socrates said. "But specifically it's bad for you. Because people get addicted to being rich, too. I mean, look at me. I had to work very hard in the past. That's like my own evolutionary history. I can't just flip a switch now."

"But you are rich. You'll always be rich."

"So I should stop now? Is that what you're saying? Does a person stop eating cookies because he's had enough sugar for the day? No, he keeps on reaching for that packet until they're all gone."

"It was a small amount."

"My small amount."

"You've got enough."

"I need more. Because you're forgetting something else. Being rich doesn't mean anything unless other people are poor."

"You need me to be poor?"

"I like the comparison. It makes me feel better."

"I thought this was about the power of example."

"Well, that, too."

And at that point, the man in the shackles just gave up and waited. Socrates sensed the surrender. Entertainment was over. He stepped back to the corner of the room and picked up the can of gas. He poured more over the guy's head while the guy bucked and struggled and cried. Then he trailed a wet line all the way to the door. He held the can upside down to chase out the last drops. He put the can on the floor and crossed the hallway and opened the front door. His guys were back from their walk. They were waiting in the cars.

There was a breeze outside, enough to make a draft inside, enough to stir the gasoline vapors and spread the smell. The wind was blowing parallel with the front of the building, creating a slight Venturi effect, sucking air out of the house the same way a spray gun sucks paint out of a reservoir. Socrates figured the whole house would burn, but he didn't care. It wasn't his.

He clicked his lighter.

It didn't work.

The serrated wheel spun free and then jammed. The flint had broken, and the fragment had seized up the mechanism. He dropped the lighter and pulled his gun. He aimed at the floor from a foot away, right at the wet line. He figured the muzzle flash would do the trick or, failing that, the heat of the bullet itself.

The breeze gusted, the vapors stirred; he pulled the trigger, and the air itself seemed to catch fire all around him, blue flames dancing and curling and twisting, connected to nothing, then connected to his clothes, to his hair, to his skin. He stood up slowly, moving, turning, ablaze, stamping a meaningless circle inside an envelope of fire. The breeze fed the flames and pulled more vapor out of the house, which fed the fire even more. Socrates made it out the door and two steps toward his car, and then he went down heavily on his front, and the wind caught the door and slammed it shut behind him.

The guy in the shackles heard the screaming, and then he heard cars driving away, and after that he heard nothing, until an hour later the occupants of the house got back. They didn't call the cops. No one thought that was a good idea. They called the shackled man's friends instead, and four of them arrived another hour later with bolt cutters. Then all five men left, stepping over the blackened lump on the driveway.

# THE BONE-HEADED LEAGUE

For once the FBI did the right thing: it sent the Anglophile to England. To London, more specifically, for a three-year posting at the embassy in Grosvenor Square. Pleasures there were extensive, and duties there were light. Most agents ran background checks on visa applicants and would-be immigrants and kept their ears to the ground on international matters, but I liaised with London's Metropolitan Police when American nationals were involved in local crimes, either as victims or witnesses or perpetrators.

I loved every minute of it, as I knew I would. I love that kind of work, I love London, I love the British way of life, I love the theater, the culture, the pubs, the pastimes, the people, the buildings, the

Thames, the fog, the rain. Even the soccer. I was expecting it to be all good, and it was all good.

Until.

I had spent a damp Wednesday morning in February helping out, as I often did, by rubber-stamping immigration paperwork, and then I was saved by a call from a sergeant at Scotland Yard, asking on behalf of his inspector that I attend a crime scene north of Wigmore Street and south of Regent's Park. On the 200 block of Baker Street, more specifically, which was enough to send a little jolt through my Anglophile heart, because every Anglophile knows that Sherlock Holmes's fictional address was 221B Baker Street. It was quite possible I would be working right underneath the great detective's fictional window.

And I was, as well as underneath many other windows, because the Met's crime scenes are always fantastically elaborate. We have *CSI* on television, where they solve everything in forty-three minutes with DNA, and the Met has scene-of-crime officers, who spend forty-three minutes closing roads and diverting pedestrians, before spending forty-three minutes shrugging themselves into Tyvek bodysuits and Tyvek booties and Tyvek hoods, before spending forty-three minutes stringing KEEP OUT tape between lampposts and fence railings, before spending forty-three minutes erecting white tents and shrouds over anything of any interest whatsoever. The result was that I found a passable imitation of a traveling circus already in situ when I got there.

There was a cordon, of course, several layers deep, and I got through them all by showing my Department of Justice credentials and by mentioning the inspector's name, which was Bradley Rose. I found the man himself stumping around on the damp sidewalk some yards south of the largest white tent. He was a short man, but substantial, with no tie and snappy eyeglasses and a shaved head. He was an old-fashioned London thief-taker, softly spoken but at the same time impatient with bullshit, which his own department provided in exasperating quantity.

He jerked his thumb at the tent and said, "Dead man."

I nodded. Obviously I wasn't surprised. Not even the Met uses tents and Tyvek for purse snatching.

He jerked his thumb again and said, "American."

I nodded again. I knew Rose was quite capable of working that out from dentistry or clothing or shoes or hairstyle or body shape, but equally I knew he would not have involved me officially without some more definitive indicator. And as if answering the unasked question he pulled two plastic evidence bags from his pocket. One contained an opened-out blue US passport, and the other contained a white business card. He handed both bags to me and jerked his thumb again and said, "From his pockets."

I knew better than to touch the evidence itself. I turned the bags this way and that and examined both items through the plastic. The passport photograph showed a sullen man, pale of skin, with hooded eyes that looked both evasive and challenging. I glanced up and Rose said, "It's probably him. The boat matches the photo, near enough."

*Boat* was a contraction of *boat race*, which was Cockney rhyming slang for face. Apples and pears, stairs; trouble and strife, wife; plates of meat, feet; and so on. I asked, "What killed him?"

"Knife under the ribs," Rose said.

The name on the passport was Ezekiah Hopkins.

Rose said, "Did you ever hear of a name like that before?"

"Hopkins?" I said.

"No, Ezekiah."

I looked up at the windows above me and said, "Yes, I did."

The place of birth was recorded as Pennsylvania, USA.

I gave the bagged passport back to Rose and looked at the business card. It was impossible to be certain without handling it, but it seemed to be a cheap item. Thin stock, no texture, plain print, no embossing. It was the kind of thing anyone can order online for a few pounds a thousand. The legend said HOPKINS, ROSS, & SPAULDING, as if there were some kind of partnership of that name. There was no indication of what business they were supposed to be in. There was a phone number on the card, with a 610 area code. Eastern Pennsylvania, but not Philly. The address on the card said simply LEBANON, PA. East of Harrisburg, as I recalled. Correct for the 610 code. I had never been there.

"Did you call the number?" I asked.

"That's your job," Rose said.

"No one will answer," I said. "A buck gets ten it's phony."

Rose gave me a long look and took out his phone. He said, "It better be phony. I don't have an international calling plan. If someone answers in America it'll cost me an arm and a leg." He pressed 001, then 610, then the next seven digits. From six feet away I heard the triumphant little phone company triplet that announced a number that didn't work. Rose clicked off and gave me the look again.

"How did you know?" he asked.

I said, "*Omne ignotum pro magnifico est.*"

"What's that?"

"Latin."

"For what?"

"Every unexplained thing seems magnificent. In other words, a good magician doesn't reveal his tricks."

"You're a magician now?"

"I'm an FBI special agent," I said. I looked up at the windows again.

Rose followed my gaze and said, "Yes, I know. Sherlock Holmes lived here."

"No, he didn't," I said. "He didn't exist. He was made up. So were these buildings. In Arthur Conan Doyle's day Baker Street only went up to about number eighty. Or one hundred, perhaps. The rest of it was a country road. Marylebone was a separate little village a mile away."

"I was born in Brixton," Rose said. "I wouldn't know anything about that."

"Conan Doyle made up the number two twenty-one," I said. "Like movies and TV make up the phone numbers you see on the screen. And the license plates on the cars. So they don't cause trouble for real people."

"What's your point?"

"I'm not sure," I said. "But you're going to have to let me have the passport. When you're done with it, I mean. Because it's probably phony, too."

"What's going on here?"

"Where do you live?"

"Hammersmith," he said.

"Does Hammersmith have a library?"

"Probably."

"Go borrow a book. *The Adventures of Sherlock Holmes.* The second story. It's called 'The Red-Headed League.' Read it tonight, and I'll come see you in the morning."

Visiting Scotland Yard is always a pleasure. It's a slice of history. It's a slice of the future, too. Scotland Yard is a very modern place these days. Plenty of information technology. Plenty of people using it.

I found Rose in his office, which was nothing more than open space defended by furniture. Like a kid's fort. He said, "I got the book but I haven't read it yet. I'm going to read it now."

He pointed to a fat paperback volume on the desk. So to give him time I took Ezekiah Hopkins's passport back to the embassy and had it tested. It was a fake, but very good, except for some blunders so obvious they had to be deliberate. Like taunts, or provocations. I got back to Scotland Yard and Rose said, "I read the story."

"And?"

"All those names were in it. Ezekiah Hopkins, and Ross, and Spaulding. And Lebanon, Pennsylvania, too. And Sherlock Holmes said the same Latin you did. He was an educated man, apparently."

"And what was the story about?"

"Decoy," Rose said. "A ruse was developed whereby a certain Mr. Wilson was regularly decoyed away from his legitimate place of business for a predictable period of time, so that an ongoing illegal task of some sensitivity could be accomplished in his absence."

"Very good," I said. "And what does the story tell us?"

"Nothing," Rose said. "Nothing at all. No one was decoying me away from my legitimate place of business. That *was* my legitimate place of business. I go wherever dead people go."

"And?"

"And if they *were* trying to decoy me away, they wouldn't leave clues beforehand, would they? They wouldn't spell it out for me in advance. I mean, what would be the point of that?"

"There might be a point," I said.

"What kind?"

I asked, "If this was just some foreigner stabbed to death on Baker Street, what would you do next?"

"Not very much, to be honest."

"Exactly. Just one of those things. But *now* what are you going to do next?"

"I'm going to find out who's yanking my chain. First step, I'm going back on scene to make sure we didn't miss any other clues."

"*Quod erat demonstrandum,*" I said.

"What's that?"

"Latin."

"For what?"

"They're decoying you out. They've succeeded in what they set out to do."

"Decoying me out from what? I don't do anything important in the office."

He insisted on going. We headed back to Baker Street. The tents were still there. The tape was still fluttering. We found no more clues. So we studied the context instead, physically, looking for the kind of serious crimes that could occur if law enforcement was distracted. We didn't find anything. That part of Baker Street had the official Sherlock Holmes museum, and the waxworks, and a bunch of stores of no real consequence, and a few banks, but the banks were all bust anyway. Blowing one up would be doing it a considerable favor.

Then Rose wanted a book that explained the various Sherlock Holmes references in greater detail, so I took him to the British Library in Bloomsbury. He spent an hour with an annotated compendium. He got sidetracked by the geographic errors Conan Doyle had made. He started to think the story he had read could be approached obliquely, as if it were written in code.

Altogether we spent the rest of the week on it. The Wednesday, the Thursday, and the Friday. Easily thirty hours. We got nowhere. We made no progress. But nothing happened. None of Rose's other cases unraveled, and London's crime did not spike. There were no consequences. None at all.

So as the weeks passed both Rose and I forgot all about the matter. And Rose never thought about it again, as far as I know. I did, of course. Because three months later it became clear that it was I who had been decoyed. My interest had been piqued, and I had spent thirty hours doing fun Anglophile things. They knew that would happen, naturally. They had planned well. They knew I would be called out to the dead American, and they knew how to stage the kinds of things that would set me off like the

Energizer Bunny. Three days. Thirty hours. Out of the building, unable to offer help with the rubber-stamping, not there to notice them paying for their kids' college educations by rubber-stamping visas that should have been rejected instantly. Which is how four particular individuals made it to the States, and which is why three hundred people died in Denver, and which is why I—unable, in the cold light of day, to prove my naive innocence—sit alone in Leavenworth in Kansas, where by chance one of the few books the prison allows is *The Adventures of Sherlock Holmes*.

# I HEARD A ROMANTIC STORY

I heard a romantic story. It was while I was waiting to kill a guy. And not just a guy, by the way. They were calling this guy a prince, and I guess he was. A lot of those guys over there are princes. Not just one or two a country. Families have princes. All kinds of families. They have princes of their own. There are hundreds of them. They have so many that some of them are twenty-five-year-old assholes. That kind of prince. And he was the target. This young asshole. He was going to show up in a large Mercedes sedan. He was going to get out of the backseat and walk about ten steps to the porch of the house. The porch was supposed to be like they have at a Marriott hotel, but smaller. Where you get out of the shuttle bus. Only they made it too small for cars. I guess it was supposed to keep the sun off people. Maybe animals. Because, by the way, this was India. It was the middle of the day and everything was scorching hot and too bright to look at. But this guy was going to walk to this porch. And the porch was kind of walled in partly. And as soon as I was sure he was moving at a consistent pace, I had to time it right so that I actually pushed the button first, and then he got to the walled part of the porch second, and of course the wall was where the bomb was. So it was just a button job. Easy enough for one guy to do. Except of course, they sent two guys. But then, they always do. No guy is ever alone. You go to the movies and you see the guy all on his own? Obviously he's not all on his own, because there's a cameraman right in his face. Otherwise you wouldn't be seeing him. There would be no movie. That's a minimum of two guys right there. And that's how it was for us. Two guys. If I was a sniper, you'd have to call this other guy the spotter. Except I wasn't a sniper. This was a button job. I didn't need a spotter. But he was there. Probably a CIA guy. He was talking to me. It was like he had to validate the hit and give his permission. Maybe they didn't want any radio snafus. So they put the guy right next to me. Right in my ear. And presumably he knows this Mercedes sedan is some distance away, and therefore some time away, and therefore his validation was not going to be required until some future period. And we could see the road, anyway. Certainly we could see the last hundred yards of it. After the turn. And we'd have seen dust clouds miles away. And we weren't seeing any, which gave this guy time to talk. And he talked about how we'd gotten as far as we had, with this prince. He laid the whole thing out. He told me how it was done, basically. Which was not complicated, by the way. It was just a number of fairly simple things. They all had to work together, and we'd get a positive result. And obviously one of the strands was the old thing with the girl, and that part was working fine. Which is what this other guy was telling me. Because he seemed to be in charge of the whole girl part of the program. He was the chief. He sent the girl. Which was obviously a matter of selection. It's about judging the task and sending the right girl. Which this guy did. I don't think there was a lack of self-confidence in his choice. The problem was the best girl for the job in his professional judgment was also the same girl he was in love with, which obviously placed him in a predicament. He had to send the girl he loved into battle. And not battle with guns and bombs. The weapons his girlfriend was going to use were considerably more personal. It was that sort of game. And the guy knew it, obviously. He was the chief. I'm not saying he invented it, by the way. I'm saying he was currently the world's leading exponent. He was the big dog. It's not a question of second-guessing the guy. He did the right thing. He was a professional. He put his country first. The girl went. And did a fine job obviously. Within two weeks the guy was heading to this house in his Mercedes. That's diligence, right there. Two weeks is a pretty short time. To get a positive result in two weeks is extraordinary. Positive in the sense that I still had to push the button. I was a strand, too. I was the final strand. All I had to do was push the button. If the guy showed up. Which he did, because of this other guy's girlfriend. She must have done all sorts of things. The guy knew that. This is what these girls do. But he's kind of denying it. That's what he's saying to me. He's making it different for her. Maybe she didn't do all these things. Or maybe she did. The guy didn't make it entirely clear to me. But if she did, it was because she was doing it for the mission, of which he was the chief. She knew he knew it was mission critical. So she did it. She delivered the guy, and I'm waiting to push my button, which is on a cell phone, by the way. Cell phones are what we use now. They built a whole network just for us to blow things up. Private capital. Providers who take complaints. With radios you couldn't complain. If something went wrong you shrugged your shoulders and you tried again the next day. But if some guy gets his call dropped, he complains. He complains real loud. Maybe it was some big deal he was doing. So the cell companies keep things working. The only drawback being the time lag. You dial a call, it's a long time before it rings. There are all kinds of towers and computers in the way. All kind of technical management. The delay can be eight whole seconds, which was why it was all about timing. I had to judge his pace so I could push the button eight whole seconds before he got where he was going. After he arrived in the car. Which wasn't happening yet, which gave the guy time to talk, which he did, mostly about this girl. She was living with him. Obviously not for the two weeks she was with the prince, which was the point of the whole conversation, which was actually a monologue on his part in that he was attempting to convince me he was okay with it. And that she was okay with him being okay with it. It was a minefield. But allegedly both of them were okay with it. This is what the guy was trying to persuade me about. While we waited. Which turned out to be for an hour, by the way. For one hour. We were in position one hour early. Which proves the guy planned to use the time talking, because he was the one who drew up the schedule and he was the one who was doing the talking. About this girl. This girl was an angel. Which I was prepared to believe. This was a hard guy to tolerate. But he told me all the stuff they did together and I couldn't help but believe they had several happy years behind them. They weren't doing new-relationship stuff anymore, but they weren't doing old-relationship stuff yet, either. They were doing normal things, happy, maybe still a little experimental, same as some people do for a long time. I was convinced. It was a convincing description. At the time I was sure it was true. Which it was, obviously. Eventually a lot of people saw it for themselves. But it was possible to see it way back. I believed the guy. He sent the girl to the prince. They've both had a great time the weekend before. They're cool with it. He's okay with it, and she's okay with everything. So they do it. Monday morning, off she goes. And that should be it. He's the chief, she's a girl in the field, there should be no contact between them. None at all. Organizationally she's lost to him now. She's gone. She might not be coming back. Because some of them don't. There have been fatalities. Hence the protocols. No personal involvement. Which they've been faking so far, but now they're going to have to do it for real. Except they don't. They sneak visits. Which is a huge off-the-charts no-no professionally. It's going to screw everything up forever. It's a double whammy. She's no longer deniable, and his cover is blown. But they did it. And not just once. They met five times. In two weeks. Five out of fourteen. That's a pretty decent fraction. Not far from one half. Which is a long time to be away. Her performance was miraculous. She got the job done in two weeks, half of which was spent back with her original boyfriend. Who was telling me all about these visits. Which was another breach of discipline right there. I mean, what was I? He should have asked for ID. But he didn't, which means he thought I was just some dumb guy who didn't matter. Which was ironic, because I was just the same as him. In fact I was exactly the same as him. I was a government operator, too. His equal in every way. Except I didn't have a girl. He was the one with the girl. And he was visiting her. The first time she was fine. She'd only just met the prince. They were still in the formal stages. The second time, not so much. They'd moved beyond the formal stages. Twenty-four lousy hours, and the prince was already doing stuff. That was totally clear. But we're talking national security here. The best kind. You blow someone up in India, you save a lot of problems later. Maybe you save the world. Obviously people like this guy and his girl have to believe this stuff. Or maybe they already believe this stuff before they join. Maybe that's why they seek out those jobs. Because they believe certain things. They believe there is something bigger than themselves. That's why the girl goes back to the prince, even after that second visit. We can guess what she's doing, because she's in a bad state when the third visit rolls around. The prince is not hitting her. This is not a physical problem. The prince might not be doing anything at all. He could be totally naive and inexperienced. He could be undemanding. There was a range of possibilities. But she had to supply his needs in a very submissive manner. Whatever they were. She had to smile and curtsy like she was the happiest girl in the world. Which is a strain, psychologically. She was not having a good time. But she went back. She was determined to complete the mission. That's the kind of person she was. Which put the chief in a permanent circular argument, of course. He couldn't stop the girl he loved because if he could he wouldn't have loved her. She would have insisted she go. He would have insisted she go. National security is a very important thing. These people believe that. They have to. So she went. And she kept on going back. She seemed stronger at the fourth visit. Better still at the fifth. She was in control now. She was doing it. She was like a boxer who just won the belt. Sure he hurts, but not much. She was like that. She was going to deliver him. She was the undisputed champion of the world. She was nearly done. She was coming home. Except maybe that boxer's hurting worse than he lets on. Maybe she was. Maybe she's tired, but she's close. So she fakes it with you. She's okay to go back. So she goes back. But part of faking was exaggerating. She's going to deliver him, but it's not going to be easy. Not like she's making out. She's going to have to offer incentives. Which she hasn't mentioned to you. Because she's exaggerating. She's telling you it's better than it is. She's in control, but not all the way. And she conceals it, so you don't know. And then you see the dust cloud miles away, and you wait, and then the Mercedes comes around the turn, the last hundred yards; it's an expensive car, but dusty, and it parks right where it should and the guy gets out of the backseat. And like a prick he leaves the door wide open behind him and just walks away, like he's the king of the world, and I'm already timing him. He's doing that kind of fit-guy hustle, which is actually slower than it looks, but I'm on it and I know exactly when I'm going to push the button. Then the girl bounds out of the car behind him, like she had dropped her pocketbook or something and was delayed for a moment, which is exactly what I think she did, because she's doing a kind of apologetic thing with the body language, a kind of I'm-an-idiot look, and then she catches up to the prince and she takes his arm in a kind of affectionate way. Almost an excited way, to be truthful, and you realize she got him there by promising him something special. In one of the rooms, perhaps. Maybe something he's never done before. They're giggling like schoolkids. They're bounding ahead. They're right there at the point where you have to hit the button. And by now the validation process is seriously screwed up. We're just babbling to each other. But we know one thing. National security is very important. It's bigger than either of us. We believe that stuff. I have to. So I hit the button. My timing was good. No reason why it wouldn't be. I had no lack of self-confidence in my estimate of speed and direction. Eight seconds. They were perfectly level with the wall when it went up. Both of them. And that was the end of the romantic story.

# MY FIRST DRUG TRIAL

Was it smart to smoke a bowl before heading to court? Probably not. The charge was possession of a major quantity, and first impressions count, and a courtroom is a theater with all eyes on just two main characters: the judge, obviously, but mostly the accused. So was it smart?

Probably not.

But what choice did I have? Obviously I had smoked a bowl the night before. A big bowl, to be honest. Because I was nervous. I wouldn't have slept without it. Not that I have tried to sleep without it, even one night in twenty years. So that hit was routine. I slept the sleep of the deeply stoned and woke up feeling normal. And looking and acting normal, I'm sure. At breakfast my wife made no adverse comment, except, "Use some Visine, honey." But it was said with no real concern. Like advice about which tie to choose. Which I was happy to have. It was a big day for me, obviously.

So I shaved and dripped the drops into my eyes, and then I showered, which on that day I found especially symbolic. Even transformational. I felt like I was hosing a waxy residue that only I could see out of my hair and off my skin. It sluiced away down the drain and left me feeling fresh and clean. A new man, again. An innocent man. I stood in the warm stream for an extra minute and for the millionth time half decided to quit. Grass is not addictive. No physical component. All within my power. And I knew I should.

That feeling lasted until I had finished combing my hair. The light in my bathroom looked cold and dull. The plain old day bore down on me. Problem is, when you've stayed at the Ritz, you don't want to go back to the Holiday Inn.

I had an hour to spare. Courts never start early. I had set the time aside to review some issues. You can't expect lawyers to spot everything. A man has to take responsibility. So I went to my study. There was a pipe on the desk. It was mostly blackened, but there were some unburned crumbs.

I opened the first file. They had given me copies of everything, of course. All the discovery materials. All the pleadings and the depositions and the witnesses. I was familiar with the facts, naturally. And objectively, they didn't look good. Any blow-dried TV analyst would sit there and say, *Things don't look good here for the accused.* But there were possibilities. Somewhere. There had to be. How many things go exactly to plan?

The unburned crumbs were fat and round. There was a lighter in the drawer. I knew that. A yellow plastic thing from a gas station. I couldn't concentrate. Not properly. Not in the way I needed to. I needed that special elevated state I knew so well. And it was within easy reach.

Irresponsible, to be high at my first drug trial.

Irresponsible, to prepare while I was feeling less than my best.

Right?

I held the crumbs in with my pinkie fingernail and knocked some ash out around it. I thumbed the lighter. The smoke tasted dry and stale. I held it in, and waited, and waited, and then the buzz was there. Just microscopically. I felt the tiny thrills, in my chest first, near my lungs. I felt each cell in my body flutter and swell. I felt the light brighten and I felt my head clear.

Unburned crumbs. Nothing should be wasted. That would be criminal.

The blow-dried analysts would say the weakness in the prosecution's case was the lab report on the substances seized. But weakness was a relative word. They would be expecting a conviction.

They would say the weakness in the defense's case was all of it.

No point in reading more.

It was a railroad, straight and true.

Nothing to do for the balance of the morning hour.

I put the pipe back on the desk. There were paper clips in a drawer. Behind me on a shelf was a china jar marked *Stash*. My brother had bought it for me. Irony, I suppose. In it was a baggie full of Long Island grass. Grown from seeds out of Amsterdam, in an abandoned potato field close enough to a bunch of Hamptons mansions to deter police helicopters. Rich guys don't like noise, unless they're making it.

I took a paper clip from the drawer and unbent it and used it to clean the bowl. Just housekeeping at that point. Like loading the dishwasher. You have to keep on top of the small tasks. I made a tiny conical heap of ash and carbon on a tissue, and then I balled up the tissue and dropped it in the trash basket. I blew through the pipe, hard, like a Pygmy warrior in the jungle. Final powdered fragments came out, and floated, and settled.

Clean.

Ready to go.

For later, of course. Because right then those old unburned crumbs were doing their job. I was an inch off the ground, feeling pretty good. For the moment. In an hour I would be sliding back to earth. Good timing. I would be clear of eye and straight of back, ready for whatever the day threw at me.

But it was going to be a long day. No doubt about that. A long, hard, pressured, unaided, uncompensated day. And there was nothing I could do about it. Not even I was dumb enough to show up at a possession trial with a baggie in my pocket. Not that there was anywhere to smoke anymore. Not in a public facility. All part of the collapse of society. No goodwill, no convenience. No joy.

I swiveled my chair and scooted toward the shelf with the jar. Just for a look. Like a promise to myself that the Ritz would be waiting for me after the day in the Holiday Inn. I took off the lid and pulled out the baggie and shook it uncrumpled. Dull green, shading brown, dry and slightly crisp. Ready for instantaneous combustion. A harsher taste that way, in my experience, but faster delivery. And time was going to count.

I decided to load the pipe there and then. So it would be ready for later. No delay. In the door, spark the lighter, relief. Timing was everything. I crumbled the bud and packed the bowl and tamped it down. I put it on the desk and licked my fingers.

Timing was everything. Granted, I shouldn't be high in court. Understood. Although how would people tell? I wasn't going to have much of a role. Not on the first day, anyway. They would all look at me from time to time, but that was all. But it was better to play it safe, agreed. But it was the gap I was worried about. The unburned crumbs were going to give it up long before I arrived downtown. Which was inefficient. Who wants twenty more minutes of misery than strictly necessary?

I picked up the lighter. No one in the world knows more than I do about how a good bud burns. The flame licks over the top layer, and it browns and blackens, and you breathe right in and hold, hold, hold, and the bud goes out again, and you hold some more, and you breathe out, and the hit is there. And you've still got ninety percent left in the bowl, untouched, just lightly seasoned. Maybe ninety-five percent. Hardly like smoking at all. Just one pass with the lighter. Merely a gesture.

And without that gesture, twenty more minutes of misery than strictly necessary.

What's a man supposed to do?

I sparked the lighter. I made the pass. I held the smoke deep inside, harsh and hot and comforting.

My wife came in.

"Jesus," she said. "Today of all days?"

So it was her fault, really. I breathed out too soon. I didn't get full value. I said, "No big deal."

"You' re an addict."

"It's not addictive."

"Emotionally," she said. "Psychologically."

Which was a woman thing, I supposed. A man has a stone in his shoe, he takes it out, right? Who walks around all day with a stone in his shoe? I said, "Nothing's going to happen for an hour or so."

She said, "You can't afford to fall asleep. You can't afford to look all spacey. You understand that, right? Please tell me you understand that."

"It was nothing," I said.

"There will be consequences," she said. "We're doing well right now. We can't afford to lose it all."

"I agree, we're doing well. We've always done well. So don't worry."

"Today of all days," she said again.

"It was nothing," I said again. I held out the pipe. "Take a look."

She took a look. Exactly as predicted. The top layer a little burned, the rest untouched but lightly seasoned. Ninety-five percent still there. A breath of fresh air. Hardly like smoking at all.

She said, "No more, okay?"

Which I absolutely would have adhered to, except she had made me waste the first precious moment. And I wanted to time it right. That was all. No more and no less. I wanted to be ready when the fat guy in the uniform called out, *All rise!* But not before. No point in being ready before. No point at all.

My wife spent a hard minute looking at me, and then she left the room again. The car service was due in about twenty minutes. The ride downtown would take another twenty. Plus another twenty milling around before we all got down to business. Total of an hour. The aborted breath would have seen me through. I was sure of that. So one more would replace it. Maybe a slightly smaller version, to account for the brief passage of time. Or maybe a slightly larger version, to compensate for the brief upset. I had been knocked off my stride. Ritual is important, and interference can be disproportionately destructive.

I sparked up again. The yellow lighter. A yellow flame, hot and pure and steady. Problem is, the second pass burns better. As if those lower seasoned layers are ready and waiting. They know their fate, and they're instantly ready to cooperate. Smoke came up in a cloud, and I had to breathe in hard to capture all of it. And second time around the bud doesn't extinguish quite so fast. It keeps on smoldering, so a second breath is necessary. Waste not, want not.

Then a third breath.

By which time I knew I was right. I was getting through the morning just fine. I had saved the day. No danger of getting sleepy. I wasn't going to look spacey. I was bright, alert, buzzing, seeing things for what they were, open to everything, magical.

I took a fourth breath, which involved the lighter again. The smoke was gray and thick and instantly satisfying. I could feel the roots of my hair growing. The follicles were thrashing with microscopic activity. I could hear my neighbors getting ready for work. Stark and absolute clarity everywhere. My spine felt like steel, warm and straight and unbending, with brain commands rushing up and down its mysterious tubular interior, fast, precise, logical, targeted.

I *was functioning.*

Functioning just *fine.*

A fourth hit, and a fifth. There was a lot of weed in the bowl. I had packed it pretty tight. A homecoming treat, remember? That had been the intention. Not really a wake-and-bake. But it was there.

So I smoked it.

I felt good in the car. How could I not? I was ready to beat the world. And capable of it. The traffic seemed to get out of the way, and all the lights were green. Whatever it takes, baby. A guy should always max himself up to the peak of his capabilities. He short-changes himself any other way. He owes himself and the world his best face, and how he gets it is his own business.

They took me in through a private door, because the public lobby was a zoo. My heels tapped on the tile, fast and rhythmic and authoritative. I was standing straight and my shoulders were back. They made me wait in a room. I could hear the crowd through the door. A low, tense buzz. They were all waiting for my entrance. Hundreds of eyes, waiting to move my way.

"Time," someone said.

I pushed open the door into the well of the court. I saw the lawyers, and the spectators, and the jury pool. I saw the defendant at his table. The fat guy in the uniform called out, "All rise!"

# WET WITH RAIN

## Great Victoria Street

B irths and deaths are in the public record. Census returns and rent
rolls and old mortgages are searchable. As are citizenship appli-
cations from all the other English-speaking countries. There are all
kinds of ancestry sites on the web. These were the factors in our favor.

Against us was a historical truth. The street had been built in
the 1960s. Fifty years ago, more or less. Within living memory.
Most of the original residents had died off, but they had families,
who must have visited, and who might remember. Children and
grandchildren, recipients of lore and legend, and therefore possibly
a problem.

But overall we counted ourselves lucky. The first owners of the house in question were long dead and had left no children. The husband had surviving siblings, but they had all gone to either Australia or Canada. The wife had a living sister, still in the neighborhood, but she was over eighty years old, and considered unreliable.

Since the original pair, the house had had five owners, most of them in the later years. We felt we had enough distance. So we went with the third variant of the second plan. Hairl Carter came with me. Hairl Carter II, technically. His father had the same name. From southeastern Missouri. His father's mother had wanted to name her firstborn Harold, but she had no more than a third-grade education and couldn't spell except phonetically. So Harold it was, phonetically. The old lady never knew it was weird. We all called her grandson Harry, which might not have pleased her.

Harry did the paperwork, which was easy enough, because we made it all Xeroxes of Xeroxes, which hides a lot of sins. I opened an account at a Washington, DC, bank, in the name of the society, and I put half a million dollars into it, and we got credit cards and a checkbook. Then we rehearsed. We prepped it, like a political debate. The same conversation, over and over again, down all the possible highways and byways. We identified weak spots, though we had no choice but to barrel through. We figured audacity would stop them thinking straight.

We flew first to London, then to Dublin in the south, and then we made the connection to Belfast on tickets that cost less than cups of coffee back home. We took a cab to the Europa Hotel, which is where we figured people like us would stay. We arranged a car with the concierge. Then we laid up and slept. We figured midmorning the next day should be zero hour.

The car was a crisp Mercedes and the driver showed no real reluctance about the address—which was second from the end of a short line of ticky-tacky row houses, bland and cheaply built, with big areas of peeling white weatherboard, which must have saved money on bricks. The roof tiles were concrete and had gone mossy. In the distance the hills were like velvet, impossibly green, but all around us the built environment was hard. There was a fine cold drizzle in the air, and the street and the sidewalk were both shiny gray.

The car waited at the curb and we opened a broken gate and walked up a short path through the front yard. Carter rang the bell and the door opened immediately. The Mercedes had not gone unnoticed. A woman looked out at us. She was solidly built, with a pale, meaty face. "Who are you?"

I said, "We're from America."

"America?"

"We came all the way to see you."

"Why?"

"Mrs. Healy, is it?" I asked, even though I knew it was. I knew all about her. I knew where she was born, how old she was, and how much her husband made. Which wasn't much. They were a month behind on practically everything. Which I hoped was going to help.

"Yes, I'm Mrs. Healy," the woman said.

"My name is John Pacino, and my colleague here is Harry Carter."

"Good morning to you both."

"You live in a very interesting house, Mrs. Healy."

She looked blank, and then craned her neck out the door and stared up at her front wall. "Do I?"

"Interesting to us, anyway."

"Why?"

"Can we tell you all about it?"

She said, "Would you like a wee cup of tea?"

"That would be lovely."

So we trooped inside, first Carter, then me, feeling a kind of preliminary satisfaction, as if our leadoff hitter had gotten on base. Nothing guaranteed, but so far so good. The air inside smelled of daily life and closed windows. A skilled analyst could have listed the ingredients from their last eight meals. All of which had been either boiled or fried, I guessed.

It wasn't the kind of household where guests get deposited in the parlor to wait. We followed the woman to the kitchen, which had drying laundry suspended on a rack. She filled a kettle and lit the stove. She said, "Tell me what's interesting about my house."

Carter said, "There's a writer we admire very much, name of Edmund Wall."

"Here?"

"In America."

"A writer?"

"A novelist. A very fine one."

"I never heard of him. But then, I don't read much."

"Here," Carter said, and he took the copies from his pocket and smoothed them on the counter. They were faked to look like Wikipedia pages. Which is trickier than people think. (Wikipedia prints different than it looks on the computer screen.)

Mrs. Healy asked, "Is he famous?"

"Not exactly," I said. "Writers don't really get famous. But he's very well respected. Among people who like his sort of thing. There's an appreciation society. That's why we're here. I'm the chairman and Mr. Carter is the general secretary."

Mrs. Healy stiffened a little, as if she thought we were trying to sell her something. "I'm sorry, but I don't want to join. I don't know him."

I said, "That's not the proposition we have for you."

"Then what is?"

"Before you, the Robinsons lived here, am I right?"

"Yes," she said.

"And before them, the Donnellys, and before them, the McLaughlins."

The woman nodded. "They all got cancer. One after the other. People started to say this was an unlucky house."

I looked concerned. "That didn't bother you? When you bought it?"

"My faith has no room for superstition."

Which was a circularity fit to make a person's head explode. It struck me mute. Carter said, "And before the McLaughlins were the McCanns, and way back at the beginning were the McKennas."

"Before my time," the woman said, uninterested, and I felt the runner on first steal second. Scoring position.

I said, "Edmund Wall was born in this house."

"Who?"

"Edmund Wall. The novelist. In America."

"No one named Wall ever lived here."

"His mother was a good friend of Mrs. McKenna. Right back at the beginning. She came to visit from America. She thought she had another month, but the baby came early."

"When?"

"The 1960s."

"In this house?"

"Upstairs in the bedroom. No time to get to the hospital."

"A baby?"

"The future Edmund Wall."

"I never heard about it. Mrs. McKenna has a sister. She never talks about it."

Which felt like the runner getting checked back. I said, "You know Mrs. McKenna's sister?"

"We have a wee chat from time to time. Sometimes I see her in the hairdressers."

"It was fifty years ago. How's her memory?"

"I should think a person would remember that kind of thing."

Carter said, "Maybe it was hushed up. It's possible Edmund's mother wasn't married."

Mrs. Healy went pale. Impropriety. Scandal. In her house. Worse than cancer. "Why are you telling me this?"

I said, "The Edmund Wall Appreciation Society wants to buy your house."

"Buy it?"

"For a museum. Well, like a living museum, really. Certainly people could visit, to see the birthplace, but we could keep his papers here too. It could be a research center."

"Do people do that?"

"Do what? Research?"

"No, visit houses where writers were born."

"All the time. Lots of writers' houses are museums. Or tourist attractions. We could make a very generous offer. Edmund Wall has many passionate supporters in America."

"How generous?"

"Best plan would be to pick out where you'd like to live next, and we'll make sure you can. Within reason, of course. Maybe a new house. They're building them all over." Then I shut up, and let temptation work its magic. Mrs. Healy went quiet. Then she started to look around her kitchen. Chipped cabinets, sagging hinges, damp air.

The kettle started to whistle.

She said, "I'll have to talk to my husband."

Which felt like the runner sliding into third ahead of the throw. Safe. Ninety feet away. Nothing guaranteed, but so far so good. In fact bloody good, as they say on those damp little islands. We were in high spirits on the way back in the Mercedes.

—

The problem was waiting for us in the Europa's lobby. An Ulsterman, maybe fifty years old, in a cheap suit, with old nicks and scars on his hands and thickening around his eyes. A former field operative, no doubt, many years in the saddle, now moved to a desk because of his age. I was familiar with the type. It was like looking in a mirror.

He said, "Can I have a word?"

We went to the bar, which was dismal and empty ahead of the lunchtime rush. The guy introduced himself as a copper, from right there in Belfast, from a unit he didn't specify, but which I guessed was Special Branch, which was the brass-knuckle wing of the old Royal Ulster Constabulary, now the Police Service of Northern Ireland. Like the FBI, with the gloves off. He said, "Would you mind telling me who you are and why you're here?"

So Carter gave him the guff about Edmund Wall, and the appreciation society, and the birthplace, but what was good enough earlier in the morning didn't sound so great in the cold light of midday. The guy checked things on his phone in real time as Carter talked, and then he said, "There are four things wrong with that story. There is no Edmund Wall, there is no appreciation society, the bank account you opened is at the branch nearest to Langley, which is CIA headquarters, and most of all, that house you're talking about was once home to Gerald McCann, who was a notorious paramilitary in his day."

Carter said nothing, and neither did I.

The guy continued, "Northern Ireland is part of the United Kingdom, you know. They won't allow unannounced activities on their own turf. So again, would you mind telling me who you are and why you're here?"

I said, "You interested in a deal?"

"What kind?"

"You want to buy a friend in a high place?"

"How high?"

"Very high."

"Where?"

"Somewhere useful to your government."

"Terms?"

"You let us get the job done first."

"Who gets killed?"

"Nobody. The Healys get a new house. That's all."

"What do you get?"

"Paid. But your new friend in the very high place gets peace of mind. For which he'll be suitably grateful, I'm sure."

"Tell me more."

"First I need to check you have your head on straight. This is not the kind of thing where you make a bunch of calls and get other people involved. This is the kind of thing where you let us do our work, and then when we're gone, you announce your new relationship as a personal coup. Or not. Maybe you'll want to keep the guy in your vest pocket."

"How many laws are you going to break?"

"None at all. We're going to buy a house. Happens every day."

"Because there's something in it, right? What did Gerald McCann leave behind?"

"You got to agree to what I said before. You got to at least nod your head. I have to be able to trust you."

"Okay, I agree," the guy said. "But I'm sticking with you all the way. We're a threesome now. Until you're done. Every minute. Until I wave you off at the airport."

"No, come with us," I said. "You can meet your new friend. At least shake hands with him. Then come back. Vest pocket or not, you'll feel better that way."

He fell for it, like I knew he would. I mean, why not? Security services love a personal coup. They love their vest pockets. They love to run people. They love to be the guy. He said, "Deal. So what's the story?"

"Once upon a time there was a young officer in the US Army. A bit of a hothead, with certain sympathies. With a certain job, at a certain time. He sold some obsolete weapons."

"To Gerald McCann?"

I nodded. "Who as far as we know never used them. Who we believe buried them under his living room floor. Meanwhile, our young officer grew up and got promoted and went into a whole different line of work. Now he wants the trail cleaned up."

"You want to buy the house so you can dig up the floor?"

I nodded again. "Can't break in and do it. Too noisy. The floors are concrete. We're going to need jackhammers. Neighbors need to think we're repairing the drains or something."

"These weapons are still traceable?"

"Weapon, singular, to be honest with you. Which I'm prepared to be, in a spot like this. Still traceable, yes. And extremely embarrassing, if it comes to light."

"Did Mrs. Healy believe you about Edmund Wall?"

"She believed us about the money. We're from America."

The guy from Special Branch said, "It takes a long time to buy a house."

It took three weeks, with all kinds of lawyer stuff, and an inspection, which was a pantomime and a farce, because what did we care? But it would have looked suspicious if we had waived it. We were supposed to be diligent stewards of the appreciation society's assets. So we commissioned it, and pretended to read it afterward. It was pretty bad, actually. For a spell I was worried the jackhammer would bring the whole place down.

We stayed in Belfast the whole three weeks. Normally we might have gone home and come back again, but not with the Special Branch copper on the scene, obviously. We had to watch him every minute. Which was easy enough, because he had to watch us every minute. We all spent three whole weeks gazing at each other and reading crap about dry rot and rising damp. Whatever that was. It rained every day.

But in the end the lawyers got it done, and I received an undramatic phone call saying the house was ours. So we picked up the key and drove over and walked around with pages from the inspection report in our hands and worried expressions on our faces—which I thought of as setting the stage. The jackhammer had to be explicable. And the neighbors were nosy as hell. They were peering out and coming over and introducing themselves in droves. They brought old Mrs. McKenna's sister, who claimed to remember the baby being born, which set off a whole lot of tutting and clucking among her audience. More people came. As a result we waited two days before we rented the jackhammer. Easier than right away, we thought. I knew how to operate it. I had taken lessons from a crew repairing Langley's secure staff lot.

The living room floor was indeed concrete, under some kind of asphalt screed, which was under a foam-backed carpet so old it had gone flat and crusty. We tore it up and saw a patch of screed that was different than the rest. It was the right size too. I smiled. Gerald McCann, taking care of business.

I asked, "What actually happened to McCann?"

The Special Branch guy said, "Murdered."

"Who by?"

"Us."

"When?"

"Before he could use this, obviously, whatever it is."

And after that, conversation was impossible, because I got the hammer started. After which the job went fast. The concrete was long on sand and short on cement. Same the world over. Concrete is a dirty business. But even so, the pit was pretty deep. More than just secure temporary storage. It felt kind of permanent. But we got to the bottom eventually, and we pulled the thing out.

It was wrapped in heavy plastic, but it was immediately recognizable. A reinforced canvas cylinder, olive green, like a half-size oil drum, with straps and buckles all over it, to keep it closed up tight, and to make it man-portable, like a backpack. A big backpack. A big, heavy backpack.

The guy from Special Branch went very quiet, and then he said, "Is that what I think it is?"

"Yes, it's what you think it is."

"Jesus Christ on a bike."

"Don't worry. The warhead is a dummy. Because our boy in uniform wasn't."

Carter said, "Warhead? What is it?"

I said nothing.

The guy from Special Branch explained, "It's an SADM. A W54 in an H-912 transport container."

"Which is what?"

"A Strategic Atomic Demolition Munition. A W54 missile warhead, which was the baby of the family, adapted to use as an explosive charge. Strap that thing to a bridge pier, and it's like dropping a thousand tons of TNT on it."

"It's nuclear?"

I said, "It weighs just over fifty pounds. Less than the bag you take on vacation. It's the nearest thing to a suitcase nuke ever built."

The guy from Special Branch said, "It is a suitcase nuke, never mind the nearest thing."

Carter said, "I never heard about them."

I said, "Developed in the 1950s. Obsolete by 1970. Paratroops were trained to jump with them, behind the lines, to blow up power stations and dams."

"With nuclear bombs?"

"They had mechanical timers. The paratroops might have gotten away."

"Might have?"

"It was a tough world back then."

"But this warhead is fake?"

"Open it up and take a look."

"I wouldn't know the difference."

"Good point," I said. "Gerald McCann obviously didn't."

The guy from Special Branch said, "I can see why my new friend wants the trail cleaned up. Selling nuclear weapons to foreign paramilitary groups? He couldn't survive that, whoever he is."

———

We put the thing in the trunk of a rented car, and drove to a quiet corner of Belfast International Airport, to a gate marked *General*

*Aviation,* which meant private jets, and we found ours, which was a Gulfstream IV, painted gray and unmarked except for a tail number. The guy from Special Branch looked a little jealous.

"Borrowed," I said. "Mostly it's used for renditions."

Now he looked a little worried.

I said, "I'm sure they hosed the blood out."

We loaded the munition on board ourselves, because there was no spare crew to help us. There was one pilot and no steward. Standard practice, in the rendition business. Better deniability. We figured the munition was about the size of a fat guy, so we strapped it upright in a seat of its own. Then we all three sat down, as far from it as we could get.

———

Ninety minutes out I went to the bathroom, and after that I steered the conversation back to rendition. I said, "These planes are modified, you know. They have some of the electronic interlocks taken out. You can open the door while you're flying, for instance. Low and slow, over the water. They threaten to throw the prisoner out. All part of softening him up ahead of time."

Then I said, "Actually, sometimes they do throw the prisoner out. On the way home, usually, after he's spilled the beans. Too much trouble to do anything else, really."

Then I said, "Which is what we're going to do with the munition. We have to. We have no way of destroying it before we land, and we can't let it suddenly reappear in the US, like it just escaped from the museum. And this is the perfect setup for corroboration.

Because there's three of us. Because we're going to get questions. He needs to know for sure. So this way I can swear I saw you two drop it out the door, and you two can swear you saw it hit the water, and you can swear I was watching you do it. We can back each other up three ways."

Which all made sense, so we went low and slow and I opened the door. Salt air howled in, freezing cold, and the plane rocked and juddered. I stepped back, and the guy from Special Branch came first, sidewinding down the aisle, with one of the transport container's straps hefted in his nicked and scarred left hand, and then came the munition itself, heavy, bobbing like a fat man in a hammock, and then came Carter, a strap in his right hand, shuffling sideways.

They got lined up, side by side at the open door, their backs to me, each with a forearm up on the bulkhead to steady himself, the munition swinging slackly and bumping the floor between them. I said, "On three," and I started counting the numbers out, and they hoisted the cylinder and began swinging it, and on three they opened their hands and the canvas straps jerked free and the cylinder sailed out in the air and was instantly whipped away by the slipstream. They kept their forearms on the bulkhead, looking out, craning, staring down, waiting for the splash, and I took out the gun I had collected from the bathroom and shot the guy from Special Branch in the lower back, not because of any sadistic tendency, but because of simple ballistics. If the slug went through and through, I wanted it to carry on into thin air, not hit the airframe.

I don't think the bullet killed the guy. But the shock changed his day. He went all weak, and his forearm gave way, and he half fell and half got sucked out into the void. No sound. Just a blurred pinwheel as the currents caught him, and then a dot that got smaller, and then a tiny splash in the blue below, indistinguishable from a million white-crested waves.

I stepped up and helped Carter wrestle the door shut. He said, "I guess he knew too much."

I said, "Way too much."

We sat down, knee to knee.

———

Carter figured it out less than an hour later. He was not a dumb guy. He said, "If the warhead was a dummy, he could spin it like entrapment, like taking a major opponent out of the game. Or like economic warfare. Like a Robin Hood thing. He took a lot of bad money out of circulation, in exchange for a useless piece of junk. He could be the secret hero. The super-modest man."

"But?" I said.

"He's not spinning it that way. And all those people died of cancer. The Robinsons, and the Donnellys, and the McLaughlins."

"So?" I said.

"The warhead was real. That was an atom bomb. He sold nuclear weapons."

"Small ones," I said. "And obsolete."

Carter didn't reply. But that wasn't the important part. The important part came five minutes later. I saw it arrive in his eyes. I said, "Ask the question."

He said, "I'd rather not."

I said, "Ask the question."

"Why was there a gun in the bathroom? The Special Branch guy was with us the whole time. You didn't call ahead for it. You had no opportunity. But it was there for you anyway. Why?"

I didn't answer.

He said, "It was there for me. The Special Branch guy was happenstance. Me, you were planning to shoot all along."

I said, "Kid, our boss sold live nuclear weapons. I'm cleaning up for him. What else do you expect?"

Carter said, "He trusts me."

"No, he doesn't."

"I would never rat him out. He's my hero."

"Gerald McCann should be your hero. He had the sense not to use the damn thing. I'm sure he was sorely tempted."

Carter didn't answer that. Getting rid of him was difficult, all on my own, but the next hours were peaceful, just me and the pilot, flying high and fast toward a spectacular sunset. I dropped my seat way back, and I stretched out. Relaxation is important. Life is short and uncertain, and it pays to make the best of whatever comes your way.

# THE TRUTH ABOUT
# WHAT HAPPENED

I came out of my deposition feeling pretty good about it. My answers were brief and concise. My control was good. I said nothing I shouldn't have said. I used an old trick someone taught me long ago, which was to count to three in my head before replying to a question. Name? One, two, three, Albert Anthony Jackson. The trick mitigates against hasty and unwise responses. Because it gives you time to think. It drives them crazy, but there's nothing they can do about it. The oath doesn't say "the truth, the whole truth, and nothing but the truth, all within three seconds of opposing counsel shutting his yap." Try it. One day it will save your ass. Because unwise responses are tempting at times. As in my case that morning. The committee chairman had a clear agenda. The very first substantive question out of his mouth was, "Why aren't you in the armed services?" As if I was a coward, or a moral degenerate of some kind. To take my credibility away, I supposed, if necessary, if the deposition ever came to light.

"I have a wooden leg," I said.

Which was true. Not from Pearl Harbor or anything. Not that I discourage the assumption. Truthfully I was run over by a Model T Ford in the state of Mississippi. A narrow wooden wheel, a hard tire, a splintered shin, a rural doctor miles from anywhere. He took the easy way out by taking the leg off below the knee. No big deal. Except the army didn't want me. Or the navy. But they wanted everyone else. Which meant by the summer of 1942 the FBI was hurting for recruits. The leg didn't worry them. Maple, like a baseball bat. Not that they asked. They gave me training and then a badge and a gun, and then they sent me out in the world.

So a year later I was armed, at least, if not in the service. But even then the guy gave no ground. He said, "I'm sorry to hear about your misfortune," disapprovingly, accusingly, as if I had been care-less, or long premeditated a plan to avoid the draft. But after that we got along fine. He stuck mainly to procedural questions about the investigation, and one, two, three. I answered them all, and I was out of the room by a quarter to twelve. Feeling pretty good, as I said, until Vanderbilt grabbed me in the corridor and told me I had to go do another one.

"Another what?" I said.

"Deposition." he said. "Although not really. No oath. No bullshit. Strictly off the record, for our own files."

I said. "Do we really want our files to be different than their files?"

"The decision has been made," Vanderbilt said. "They want the truth to be recorded somewhere."

He took me to a different room, where we waited for twenty minutes, and then a stenographer came in, ready to take notes. She was an ample, hard-bodied thing. Maybe thirty. Brassy blonde hair. I figured she would look good in a bathing suit. She didn't want to talk. Then Slaughter came in. Vanderbilt's boss. He claimed to be related to Enos Slaughter of the St. Louis Cardinals, but no one believed him.

We all sat down, and Slaughter waited until the hardbody had her pencil poised and then he said, "OK, tell us the story."

I said. "All of it?"

"For our own internal purposes."

"It was Mr. Hopper's idea," I said.

Always better to get the blame in early.

"This is not a witch hunt," Slaughter said. "Start at the beginning. Your name. For posterity."

One, two, three.

"Albert Anthony Jackson," I said.

"Position?"

"I'm an FBI special agent temporarily detached for the duration."

"To where?"

"Where we are right now," I said.

"Which is what?"

"The project," I said.

"State its name, for the record."

"The Development of Materials Group."

"Its new name."

"Are we even allowed to say it?"

"Relax, Jackson, will you?" Slaughter said. "You're among friends. You're not under oath. You don't have to sign anything. All we want is an oral history."

"Why?"

"We won't be flavor of the month forever. Sooner or later they'll turn on us."

"Why would they?"

Vanderbilt said, "Because we're going to win this thing for them. And they don't like to share the spotlight."

"I see," I said.

"So we better have our own version ready."

Slaughter said, "State the name of the project."

I said, "The Manhattan Project."

"Your duties?"

"Security."

"Successful?"

"So far."

"What did Mr. Hopper ask you to do?"

"He didn't, at first," I said. "It started out routine. They needed another facility built. In Tennessee. A lot of concrete. A lot of specialist engineering. The budget was two hundred million dollars. They needed a man in charge. My job was to run the vetting process."

"Tell us what that involves."

"We look for embarrassing things in their personal lives and suspicious things in their politics."

"Why?"

"We don't want them to be blackmailed for secrets, and we sure as hell don't want them to give secrets away for free."

"Who were you investigating on this occasion?"

"A man named Sherman Bryon. He was a structural engineer. An old guy, but he could still get things done. The idea was to make him a colonel in the army and put him to work. If he came up clean."

"And did he?"

"At first he was fine. I got a look at him, at a meeting about something else entirely. Concrete ships, as a matter of fact. I like to get a look at a guy first. From a distance, when he doesn't know. Tall guy, well dressed, silver hair, silver mustache. Old, but erect. Probably very well spoken. That kind of guy. Patrician, they call it. There was nothing on paper. He voted against FDR all three times, but we like that, officially. No leftist sympathies. Considered to be a seal of approval. No financial worries. No professional scandals. None of his structures ever fell down."

"But?"

"Next step was to talk to his friends. Or listen to them, actually. To what they say, and what they don't."

"And what did you hear?"

"Not much, initially. Those type of people are very discreet. Very proper. They talked to me like they would talk to the mailman. They were polite and I was left in no doubt. I worked for a solid and useful organization, but they weren't about to share confidences."

"How do you get around a thing like that?"

"We tell part of the truth. But not all of it. I hinted there was a top-secret project. War work. National security. Concrete ships, I hinted, absolutely vital. I told them these days sharing confidences was a patriotic duty."

"And?"

"They loosened up some. They like the guy. And respect him. Businesswise he's a straight shooter. He pays his bills. He treats his people well. He's very successful in a high-end niche."

"All good, then."

"There was something they weren't saying. I had to push."

"And?"

"Old Sherman is married. But there are stories about a piece on the side. Apparently he's been seen with her."

"Did you classify that as a blackmail risk?"

"I went to see Mr. Hopper," I said.

"Who is, for posterity?"

"My boss. Director of Security. It was a big decision. Mr. Hopper especially liked the part about being a success in a high-end niche. He was thinking about making him a brigadier general, not a colonel. He was the exact type of guy we needed. To pass on him would be a big step to take."

"Did Mr. Hopper think blackmail was likely?"

"Not really. But where do you draw the line?"

"Did you advise Mr. Hopper one way or the other?"

"I said we should get more information. I said we shouldn't take a big step based on rumor alone."

"Did Mr. Hopper listen to your advice?"

"Maybe. He's not a stuck-up guy. He's got time for us all. Or maybe he agreed with me anyhow. Or maybe he's getting gun-shy about going to meetings and putting a wrench in their gears. Maybe he wanted to put it off. But whichever, he said he wanted more information."

"How did you go about getting it?"

"There was nothing I could do for the first three days. Old Sherman wasn't seeing either one of his women. He was stuck in a concrete boat conference. I mean, do you think they could possibly work?"

"Do I?" Slaughter said. "Concrete boats?"

"Sounds like a dumb idea to me."

"I'm not a nautical expert."

"It's not like steel plate. They'd have to mold it real thick."

"Can we stay on the subject?"

"Sorry. The guy was in the boat conference. He was working hard. He wasn't spending the day between the sheets. But Mr. Hopper wanted to see it with his own eyes. He really liked the guy. Liked him for the job, I mean. He wanted no doubt about it. So we had to wait."

"How long?"

"We spread a little grease around. Hotels, mostly. We got a call from a clerk that old Sherman had booked a room for Friday night. A double. The names given were him and his wife. Which no one believed. Why book a hotel? They have a house. So Mr. Hopper made a plan."

"Which was?"

"First we went to look at the hotel. Mr. Hopper wanted to do it in the lobby. He felt the bedroom was wrong, for that type of guy.

So we measured it up. There were gray velvet armchairs, three on one side and two on the other. There was a reception hutch, all heavy carved oak. There was a curtained doorway to the breakfast room. Mr. Hopper figured out how he wanted to do it. There was a window. To the right of the door. A person on tiptoe could see in from the street. Which was good, except it wasn't really. He couldn't spend hours peering in at the window. Not out there on the sidewalk. Passersby would tell a cop. He would have to time it just right. He couldn't see a way around it."

"How did he solve the problem?"

"He didn't. I suggested I take over from the reception clerk for a couple of days. Like an undercover role. I figured I wouldn't have much to do. I figured I could hide behind the lampshade most of the time. No one would be looking at me. So I figured I could flash the outside neon when the time came for Mr. Hopper to take a peek. The switch is right there."

"Your idea was you would alert him as they were checking in together?"

"We figured it would work two separate ways. He would get the visual he wanted, and I would see the girlfriend signing in as the wife, up close and personal. Mr. Hopper wasn't happy, because he liked the guy, as I said, but he had to draw the line somewhere. This project is a big deal."

"Did the plan work?"

"No." I said. "It really was his wife. She showed me her driver's license. Kind of automatically. I guess she travels with him a lot. To all those secure conferences about concrete boats. So she does it without thinking. The name was right and the photograph was right."

"So what did you do?"

"Nothing. I played at being a hotel clerk. Then the phone rang and it was Mr. Hopper in a booth across the street. Urgent. We had a tip the other woman was on her way to the same hotel. Right then. Mr. Hopper told me to stand by. I was to get old Sherman to come downstairs. Which I figured wouldn't be a problem. He wouldn't want me to send her up. Not with his wife in the room."

"Did the woman arrive?"

"It was like something in a motion picture. One of those screwball comedies. I heard the elevator moving. It was between me and the breakfast room. The gate opens and out steps old Sherman. He's carrying his wife's fur wrap. She steps out right behind him. In a blue dress, carrying a magazine. Half of me is thinking like an agent, and half of me is thinking, Come on, pal, get the hell out of here before it's too late. But the wife sits down in a chair, right in front of me. She starts reading her magazine. Old Sherman just stands there, two steps from the elevator. By this point I'm hiding behind the lampshade. Then the other woman walks in. Fur coat, fur hat, a red dress. An older woman. Sherman's age. She bends down and kisses the wife on the cheek and then walks over and does the same thing to Sherman. I'm thinking, What have we got here? Three in a bed? That would be worse."

"What happened next?"

"The other woman sat down, and the wife kept on reading. The other woman looked up and said something to Sherman. Polite conversation ensued. I flashed the neon and I saw Mr. Hopper look in the window. He saw it all. He remembers all the details. The painting on the wall, of a mountain lake. But he couldn't make sense of what was happening. He didn't know what the scene was about."

"What did he do?"

"He stood down and waited on the sidewalk. Old Sherman left with his wife. The other woman stayed behind and asked me to call her a taxi. I took the initiative and showed her my badge, and I gave her the same spiel I gave his friends. National security, and all that. I asked her some questions."

"And?"

"She's old Sherman's mother-in-law. Younger than him by two years, but that's how the cookie crumbles. Old Sherman is very happy with his child bride. She's very happy with him. The mother-in-law is happy with them both. She's visiting for a month and he's showing her around. She thinks he's sweet to take the time. We think he's doing it to please his wife. And she's worth pleasing. Especially for an old guy. They were in the hotel not their house because they had an early train. So panic over. Plenty of men marry younger women. No law against it. Mr. Hopper passed him fit for the job, and he's out there in Tennessee already, making a start."

Slaughter paused a bear, and then he said, "OK, I think we have what we need. Thanks, Jackson."

So for the second time that clay I came out of a deposition feeling pretty good about it. I had said nothing I didn't want to say. Some of the truth was recorded. Everyone was happy. We won it for them in the end. Then they turned on us. But old Sherman Bryon was dead by then, so it didn't matter.

# PIERRE, LUCIEN, AND ME

I survived my first heart attack. But as soon as I was well enough to sit up in bed, the doctor came back and told me I was sure to have a second. Only a matter of time, he said. The first episode had been indicative of a serious underlying weakness. Which it had just made worse. Could be days. Or weeks. Months at most. He said from now on I should consider myself an invalid.

I said, "This is 1928, for fuck's sake. They got people talking on the radio from far away. Don't you have a pill for it?"

No pill, he said. Nothing to be done. Maybe see a show. And maybe write some letters. He told me what people regretted most were the things they didn't say. Then he left. Then I left. Now I have been home four days. Doing nothing. Just waiting for the second episode. Days away, or weeks, or months. I have no way of knowing.

I haven't been to see a show. Not yet. I have to admit it's tempting. Sometimes I wonder if the doctor had more in mind than entertainment. I can imagine choosing a brand new musical, full of color and spectacle and riotous excitement, with a huge finale, whereupon all of us in the audience would jump to our feet for a standing ovation, and I would feel the clamp in my chest, and fall to the floor like an empty raincoat slipping off an upturned seat. I would die there while the oblivious crowd stamped and cheered all around me. My last hours would be full of singing and dancing. Not a bad way to go. But knowing my luck it would happen too soon. Some earlier stimulus would trigger it. Maybe coming up out of the subway. On the steep iron-bound stairs to the 42nd Street sidewalk. I would fall and slip back a yard, in the wet and the dirt and the grit, and people would look away and step around me, like I was a regular bum. Or I might make it to the theater and die on the stairs to the balcony. I no longer have the money for an orchestra seat. Or I might make it to the gods, clinging to the stair rail, out of breath, my heart thumping, and then keel over while the band was still tuning up. The last thing I would hear would be the keening of violin strings all aiming for concert pitch. Not good. And it might spoil things for everyone else. The performance might be canceled.

So in words I have always used, but which are now increasingly meaningless, a show is something I might do later.

I haven't written any letters, either. I know what the doctor was getting at. Maybe the last word you had with someone was a hard word. Maybe you never took the time to say, hey, you're a real good friend, you know that? But I would plead innocent to those charges. I'm a straightforward guy. Usually I talk a lot. People know what I think. We all had good times together. I don't want to spoil them by sending out some kind of a morbid goodbye message.

So why would anyone write letters?

Maybe they feel guilty about something.

Which I don't. Mostly. Hardly at all. I would never claim a blameless life, but I played by the rules. The field was level. They were crooks too. So I never laid awake at night. Still don't. I have no big thing to put right. No small thing, either. Nothing on my mind.

Except maybe, just possibly, if you pushed me really hard, I might say the Porterfield kid. He's on my mind a little bit. Even though it was purely business as usual. A fool and his money. Young Porterfield was plenty of one and had plenty of the other. He was the son of what the scandal sheets used to call a Pittsburgh titan. The old guy turned his steel fortune into an even bigger oil fortune and made all his children millionaires. They all built mansions up and down Fifth Avenue. They all wanted stuff on their walls. Dumb fucks, all of them. Except mine, who was a sweet dumb fuck.

I first met him nine years ago, late in 1919. Renoir had just died in France. It came over the telegraph. I was working at the Metropolitan Museum at the time, but only on the loading dock. Nothing glamorous, but I was hoping to work my way up. I knew some stuff, even back then. I was rooming with an Italian guy named Angelo, who wanted to be a nightclub performer. Meantime he was waiting tables at a chophouse near the Stock Exchange. One lunchtime a quartet of rich guys showed up. Fur collars, leather boots. Millions and millions of dollars, right there on the hoof. All young, like princes. Angelo overhead one of them say it was better to buy art while the artist was still alive, because the price would rise sharply when he was dead. It always did. Market forces. Supply and demand. Plus enhanced mystique and status. In response a second guy said in that case they'd all missed the boat on Renoir. The guy had seen the news ticker. But a third guy, who turned out to be Porterfield, said maybe there was still time. Maybe the market wouldn't react overnight. Maybe there would be a grace period, before prices went up.

Then for some dumb reason Angelo buttonholed Porterfield on his way out and said he roomed with a guy who worked for the Metropolitan Museum, and knew a lot about Renoir, and was an expert at finding paintings in unlikely places.

When Angelo told me that night I asked him, "Why the fuck did you say that?"

"Because we're friends," he said. "Because we're going places. You'd do the same for me. If you overheard a guy looking for a singer, you'd tell him about me, right? You help me, I help you. Up the ladder we go. Because of our talents. And luck. Like today. The rich man was talking about art, and you work at the Metropolitan Museum. Which part of that was not true?"

"I unload wagons," I said. "Crates are all I see."

"You're starting at the bottom. You're working your way up. Which ain't easy. We all know that. So you should skip the stairs and take the elevator whenever you can. The chance doesn't come often. This guy is the perfect mark."

"I'm not ready."

"You know about Renoir."

"Not enough."

"Yes enough," Angelo said. "You know the movement. You have a good eye."

Which was generous. But also slightly true, I supposed. I had seen reproductions in the newspaper. Mostly I liked older stuff, but I always tried to keep up. I could tell a Manet from a Monet.

Angelo said, "What's the worst fucking thing could happen?"

And sure enough, the next morning a messenger from the museum's mail room came out into the cold to find me and give me a note. It was a nice-looking item, on heavy stock, in a thick envelope. It was from Porterfield. He was inviting me to come over at my earliest convenience, to discuss an important proposition.

His place was ten blocks south, on Fifth, accessed through bronze gates that probably came from some ancient palace in Florence, Italy. Shipped over in a big-bellied boat, maybe along with the right kind of workers. I was shown to a library. Porterfield came in five minutes later. He was twenty-two at the time, full of pep and energy, with a big dumb smile on his big pink face. He reminded me of a puppy my cousin once had. Big feet, slipping and sliding, always eager. We waited for a man to bring us coffee, and then Porterfield told me about his grace-period theory. He said he had always liked Renoir, and he wanted one. Or two, or three. It would mean a lot to him. He wanted me to go to France and see what I could find. His budget was generous. He would give me letters of introduction for the local banks. I would be his purchasing agent. He would send me second class on the first steamship out. He would meet all my legitimate expenses. He talked and talked. I listened and listened. I figured he was about eighty percent the same as any other rich jerk in town, with too much bare wallpaper in his dining room. But I got the feeling some small part of him really liked Renoir. Maybe as more than an investment.

Eventually he stopped talking, and for some dumb reason I said, "OK, I'll do it. I'll leave right away."

Six days later I was in Paris.

It was hopeless. I knew nothing and no one. I went to galleries like a regular customer, but Renoir prices were already sky high. There was no grace period. The first guy in the chophouse had been right. Not Porterfield. But I felt duty bound, so I kept at it. I picked up gossip. Some dealers were worried Renoir's kids would flood the market with canvases found in his studio. Apparently they were stacked six deep against the walls. The studio was in a place called Cagnes-sur-Mer, which was in the hills behind Cannes, which was a small fishing port way in the south. On the Mediterranean Sea. A person could get to Cannes by train, and then probably a donkey cart could take him onward.

I went. Why not? The alternative was passage home, to a job I was sure was already gone. I was absent without leave. So I took the sleeper train, to a hot and tawny landscape. A pony and trap took me into the hills. Renoir's place was a pleasant spread. A bunch of manicured acres, and a low stone house. He had been successful for many years. No kind of a starving artist. Not anymore.

There was no one home, except a young man who said he was a good friend of Renoir's. He said his name was Lucien Mignon. He said he lived there. He said he was a fellow artist. He said Renoir's kids had been and gone, and Renoir's wife was in Nice, staying with a friend.

He spoke English, so I made sure he would pass on all kinds of sincere condolences to the appropriate parties. From Renoir's admirers in New York. Of which there were many. Who would all like to know, for reasons I made sound purely academic and even sentimental, exactly how many more paintings were left in the studio?

I figured Mignon would answer, being an artist, and therefore having a keen eye for a buck, but he didn't answer. Not directly. Instead he told me about his own life. He was a painter, at first an admirer of Renoir, then a friend, then a constant companion. Like a younger brother. He had lived in the house for ten years. He felt despite the difference in their ages, he and Renoir had formed a very deep bond. A true connection.

It sounded weird to me. Like why people get sent to Bellevue. Then it got worse. He showed me his work. It was just like Renoir's. Almost exactly copied, in style and manner and subject. All of it was unsigned, too, as if to preserve the illusion it might be the master's own product. It was a very odd and slavish homage.

The studio was a big, tall, square room. It was cool and light. Some of Renoir's work was hung on the wall, and some of Mignon's was hung beside it. It was hard to tell the difference. Below the pieces on display, there were indeed canvases stacked six deep against the walls. Mignon said Renoir's kids had set them aside. As their inheritance. They were not to be looked at and not to be touched. Because they were all very good.

He said it in a way that suggested somehow he had helped make them all very good.

I asked him if he knew of any other canvases as yet unspoken for. Anywhere in France. In answer he pointed across the room. Against another wall was a very small number of items the kids had rejected. Easy to see why. They were all sketches or experiments or otherwise unfinished. One was nothing more than a wavy green stripe running left to right across a bare canvas. Maybe a landscape, started and immediately abandoned. Mignon told me Renoir didn't really like working out of doors. He liked being inside, with his models. Pink and round. Village girls, mostly. Apparently one of them had become Mrs. Renoir.

One of the rejected canvases had the lower half of a landscape on it. A couple dozen green brushstrokes, nicely done, suggestive, but a little tentative and half-hearted. There was no sky. Another abandoned start. A canvas laid aside. But a canvas later grabbed up for another purpose. Where the sky should have been was a still life of pink flowers in a green glass vase. It was in the top left of the frame, painted sideways onto the unfinished landscape, not more than about eight inches by ten. The flowers were roses and anemones. The pink colors were Renoir's trademark. Mignon and I agreed no one did pink better than Renoir. The vase was a cheap thing, bought for a few sous at the market, or made at home by pouring six inches of boiling water into an empty wine bottle, and then tapping it with a hammer.

It was a beautiful little fragment. It looked done with joy. Mignon told me there was a nice story behind it. One summer day Mrs. Renoir had gone out in the garden to pick a bouquet. She had filled the vase with water from the pump, and arranged the stems artfully, and carried it into the house through the studio door, which was the easiest way. Her husband had seen it and was seized with desire to paint it. Literally seized, Mignon said. Such was the artistic temperament. Renoir had stopped what he was doing, and grabbed the nearest available canvas, which happened to be the unfinished landscape, and he had stood it vertically on his easel, and painted the flowers in the blank space where the sky should have been. He said he couldn't resist their wild disarray. His wife, who had spent more than ten minutes on the arrangement, smiled and said nothing.

Naturally I proposed a deal.

I said if I could take the tiny still life for myself, purely as a personal token and souvenir, then I would buy twenty of Mignon's works to sell in New York. I offered him a hundred thousand dollars of Porterfield's money.

Naturally Mignon said yes.

One more thing, I said. He had to help me cut the flowers out of the larger canvas and tack the fragment to stretchers of its own. Like a miniature original.

He said he would.

One more thing, I said. He had to paint Renoir's signature on it. Purely for my own satisfaction.

He hesitated.

I said he knew Renoir had painted it. He knew that for sure. He had watched it happen. So where was the deception?

He agreed fast enough to make me optimistic about my future.

We took the half-landscape, half-flowers canvas off its stretchers, and we cut the relevant eight-by-ten rectangle out of it, plus enough wraparound margin to fix it to a frame of its own, which Mignon assembled from wood and nails lying around. We put it all together, and then he squeezed a dot of paint from a tube, dark brown not black, and he took a fine camel hair brush and painted Renoir's name in the bottom right corner. Just *Renoir*, with a stylized first capital, and then flowing lower-case letters after it, very French, and very identical to the dozens of examples of the real thing I could see all around.

Then I chose twenty of his own canvases. Naturally I picked the most impressive and Renoir-like. I wrote him a check—*one hundred thousand and 00/100*—and we wrapped the twenty-one packages in paper, and we loaded them into the pony cart, which had waited for me, per my instructions and Porterfield's generous tip. I drove off with a wave.

I never saw Mignon again. But we stayed in business together, in a manner of speaking, for three more years.

I took a room in Cannes, in a fine seafront hotel. Bell boys brought up my packages. I went out and found an art store and bought a tube of dark brown oil, and a fine camel hair brush. I propped my little still life on the dresser and copied Renoir's signature, twenty separate times, in the bottom right corners of Mignon's work. Then I went down to the lobby and cabled Porterfield: *Bought three superb Renoirs for a hundred thousand. Returning directly.*

I was home seven days later. First stop was a framers for my still life, which I then propped on my mantelpiece, and second stop was Porterfield's mansion on Fifth, with three of Mignon's finest.

Which was where the seed of guilt was planted. Porterfield was so fucking happy. So fucking delighted. He had his Renoirs. He beamed and smiled like a kid on Christmas morning. They were fabulous, he said. They were a steal. Thirty-three grand apiece. He even gave me a bonus.

I got over it pretty fast. I had to. I had seventeen more Renoirs to sell, which I did, leaking them out slowly over a three-year span, to preserve their value. I was like the dealers I had met in Paris. I didn't want a glut. With the money I got I moved uptown. I never lived with Angelo again. I met a guy who said RCA stock was the thing to buy, so I did, but I got taken for a ride. I lost most everything. Not that I could complain. The biter bit, and so on. Sauce for the fucking goose. My world shrunk down to a solitary life in the uncaring city, buoyed up by the glow of my roses and anemones above the fireplace. I imagined the same feeling inside Porterfield's place, like two pins in a map. Twin centers of happiness and delight. He with his Renoirs, and me with mine.

Then the heart attack, and the guilt. The sweet dumb fuck. The big smile on his face. I didn't write a letter. How could I explain? Instead I took my Renoir off the wall, and wrapped it in paper, and walked it up Fifth, and through the bronze Italian gates, to the door. Porterfield wasn't home. Which was OK. I gave the package to his flunky, and said I wanted his boss to have it, because I knew he liked Renoir. Then I walked away, back to my place, where I continue to sit, just waiting for the second episode. My wall looks bare, but maybe better for it.

# NEW BLANK DOCUMENT

This all was about ten years ago, back when I didn't get many cold calls at all. Maybe I would get two in a month. Sometimes three. Random assignments, because I was cheap, and I was always available. I was a new freelancer making his name, fully aware that for a long time pickings would be slim, so I was also always willing. I was happy to go anywhere and do anything. A couple thousand words here or there would pay my rent. Another couple thousand would put food on my table.

My phone rang and I answered it and heard faint whistling and scratching. Not a local number. Turned out to be a magazine editor in Paris, France. A transatlantic call. The first I ever got. The guy's English was accented but fluent. He said he had gotten my name from a bureau. The place he mentioned was one we all signed up for, in the hopes of getting a little local legwork for a foreign publication. Turned out my hopes had come true that day. The guy in Paris said he wanted to send me on just such an assignment. He said his magazine was the biggest this and the biggest that, but in the end what it boiled down to for me was he wanted sidebar coverage about some guy's brother.

"Cuthbert Jackson's brother," he said, reverently, like he was awarding me the Nobel Prize for Literature.

I didn't answer. I pecked out *Cuthbert Jackson* one-handed on my keyboard, and the search engine came back with an obscure American jazz pianist, an old black guy, born in Florida but for a long time permanently resident in France.

I said, "Cuthbert Jackson the piano player?"

"And so much more," the Paris guy said. "You know him, of course. My magazine is attempting a full-scale biography. We plan to serialize it over thirteen weeks. Recently, for the first time ever, Monsieur Jackson revealed he has a living relative. A brother, still in Florida. Naturally we need to include his point of view in our story. You must go see him at once. Am I correct you live near Florida?"

As a matter of fact he was correct, which I guess explained how he picked me out of the bureau's list. Simple geography. Less mileage.

I said, "Florida is a big state, but yes, I live right next to it."

"Ideally you should obtain biographical detail about their family situation. That would be excellent. But don't worry. Worst case, we can use anything you get, as purely sidebar coverage if necessary, as if to say, by the way, Monsieur Jackson has a brother, and this is where he's living, and this is what he's doing."

"I understand," I said.

"This is very important."

"I understand," I said again.

———

Ten years ago the net was not what it is today. But it was far enough along to give me what I needed. There were message boards and fan forums, and websites with old photographs, and jazz history sites, and some political stuff, mostly in French. Long story short, Cuthbert Jackson was born in 1925 in a no-account shit-hole in the Florida Panhandle. There was one piano in town and he played it all the time. He was such a prodigy that by the time he was four people were so used to it they stopped mentioning it. At the age of eighteen he was drafted by the US Army and trained up as a support engineer. He was sent to Europe with the D-Day invasion. He was sent to Paris to march in the GI parade after liberation. He never left. At first he was listed as AWOL, and then he was forgotten about.

He played the piano in Paris, all through the grim postwar years, sweating in tiny downstairs clubs, for people desperate for something new to believe in, who found part of it in American music played by an exiled black man. He would have said he was evolving the music, not just playing it, perhaps faster and more radically because of his isolation. He wasn't in LA or Greenwich Village. He wasn't really hearing anyone else's stuff. Which made some folks call his direction a school or a movement, which led to existential disputes with devotees of other schools and movements. Which led to growing fame, which in an adopted French way made him more and more reclusive, which made him more and more famous. What little he said, he considered plain common sense, but when translated into French he sounded like Socrates. His record sales went through the roof. In France. Nowhere else. It was a thing back then. There were black writers and poets and painters, all Americans, all living in Paris, all doing well. News weeklies did a couple of stories. Cuthbert Jackson's name came up.

Because of the political stuff. France was moving right along. It had aerospace and automobiles and nuclear bombs. Everyone was doing pretty well. Except Americans were doing better. Which led to a heady mixture of disdain and envy. Which led to criticism. Which led to a question: Why do your black people do better when they come over here?

Which was kind of smug, and totally circular, because it wasn't really a question, but a move in the game. Either way it was buried by the gigantic storms already brewing at home. By contrast it seemed quaint and civilized. People agreed a movie could be made. People wondered if a State Department memo could be optioned.

Cuthbert Jackson himself generally ignored the issue, but if asked a direct question, he would answer, with what he considered plain common sense, though as he got older and terser the French translations came out more and more weird and philosophical. One guy wrote a whole book about Jackson's five-word answer to a question about the likely future of mankind.

His most recent CD was with his regular trio, and it had sold pretty well.

His most recent public statement was that he had a brother.

———

On my map the address everyone seemed to agree on looked to be in hardscrabble country, most of a day's drive away, so I left early. I was sure there would be no motels. I figured I would sleep in the car. Anything and anywhere. I had rent to pay.

The town was as bad as I had expected. Maybe a little meaner. It was all low houses, grouped tight around what looked like the archaeological ruins of a previous civilization. Some kind of an old factory, maybe sugar, and the stores and the banks that followed, some in decent buildings, even handsome, in a modest, three-story kind of way, all abandoned decades ago, now overgrown and falling down. I got out of the car where I saw a group of men gathered. They were all waiting for something. There was a mixture of impatience for it and certainty it would arrive.

I asked a guy, "What's coming?"

He said, "The pizza truck."

It showed up right on time and turned out to be their new version of a bar, since their last real bar fell down. The pizza guy had cans of beer in a cooler, which might or might not have complied with county ordinances, but which either way turned eating pizza into a standing-around event, like the best kind of place, with the beer playing the role of the beer, and the pizza standing in for the potato chips and the salted peanuts. I counted twenty people. I told one of them I was looking for Cuthbert Jackson's brother.

He said, "Who?"

"Cuthbert Jackson. He played the piano. He had a brother."

Another guy said, "Who?"

And then another. They all seemed interested. Maybe they ran out of things to say about pizza.

I said, "He's famous in France."

No reaction.

I asked, "Who is the oldest person here?"

Turned out to be a guy aged eighty, eating a pepperoni pie and drinking a High Life.

I asked him, "Do you remember World War Two?"

He said, "Sure I do."

"Cuthbert Jackson went in the army when he was eighteen, which would make you sixteen at the time. Prior to that he could play the piano real well. You probably heard him."

"That kid never came back."

"Because he stayed in France."

"We thought he was killed."

"He wasn't. Now he says he has a brother."

"Is he still a musician?"

"Very much so."

"Then maybe it's a metaphor. You know what it's like, with artistic people. Maybe he had some kind of spiritual epiphany. All about the brotherhood of man."

"Suppose he didn't?"

"Are you a reporter?"

"Proud to be," I said, like I always planned to.

"Who do you work for?"

"Anyone prepared to pay me. Right now a magazine in France."

The guy said, "We thought he was killed. Why would he stay in France? I don't see how that's natural."

I said, "Do you know his brother?"

"Sure," he said, and he walked me a couple of steps, and waved the pointed end of his pepperoni pie at the last house on the next street.

---

I knocked on the door, and it was opened by another guy who looked about eighty. Which was about right. Cuthbert himself was eighty-two. His long-lost brother would be plus or minus. The old guy said his name was Albert Jackson. I told him a guy from these parts named Cuthbert Jackson had become very famous in France. Recently he had added to his bio that he had a brother.

"Why would he say that?" Albert asked.

"Is it not true?"

"On the television shows they want the truth, the whole truth, and nothing but the truth."

"I'm just a reporter asking a question."

"What was the question?"

"Are you Cuthbert Jackson's brother?"

Albert Jackson said, "Yes, I am."

"That's good."

"Is it?"

"In the sense that the new bio is proved correct. Future historians will not be misled. In France, I mean. A guy wrote a whole book about five words he said."

"I haven't seen him for more than sixty years."

"What do you remember of him?"

"He could play the piano."

"Did you think he was killed in the war?"

Albert shook his head. "He told me many times. He was going to let them take him all over, and he was going to pick out the best place he saw, and he was going to stay there. He said if the war lasted long enough for me to get drafted, I should do the same thing."

"Because it would be better somewhere else for a black man?"

"Who plays the piano, I guess. Although plenty of piano-playing folk are doing pretty good right here."

"Did you ever hear from him?"

"One time. I wrote him about something, and he wrote me back."

"Were you surprised he never came home?"

"I guess a little at first. But later, not so much."

"Would you help me out with background information about your family situation?"

"I guess someone needs to."

"Why's that?"

"You think the bio is correct, but it ain't. Historians will be wrong. I don't know why he said what he said, that he had a brother. I'm not sure what he meant. I might want some time to figure it out."

"I don't understand. You just told me you and he are brothers."

"We are."

"Then what's the problem?"

"The bio should say he had two brothers."

We sat down and I took out my computer, and Albert started to tell me the story, but as soon as I saw where it was going, I paused him momentarily, and saved the French file, and opened a new blank document, for what I felt was going to be the real story. I remember the moment. It felt like journalists ought to feel.

A black farmer named Bertrand Jackson had three sons and three daughters, all thirty months apart, all perfectly interlaced in terms of gender, Cuthbert first, the eldest boy, who grew up playing the piano, then went to war, then stayed overseas. The middle boy was Albert, sitting right there telling me the story, and the youngest boy was Robert. The girls in between were delightful. Their mother was happy. The land was producing. Things were pretty good for the farmer. He felt like a man of substance. Altogether a success. He had only one problem. His youngest son, Robert, was slow in the head. He was always smiling, always amiable, but farm work was beyond him. Which was okay. The others could carry him.

Then the farmer made a mistake. Because he felt like a man of substance, he tried to register to vote in the presidential election. He felt it was his civic duty. He kept on going a good long time before he gave up. Afterward a county guy told him never to try again. Things got chilly. They were jealous, he figured. Because his farm was doing well. Maybe a little disconcerted. November rolled into December.

Meanwhile the farmer had gotten Robert a job sweeping up in the dry goods store where he bought his seed. The owner was a white guy. Sometimes his daughter worked the register. Christmas was coming, so Robert made her a card. He labored over the writing. He put, *I hope you send me a card too.* Her daddy saw it, and he showed it to his friends, and pretty soon a lynch mob was coming for Robert, because of his lewd interracial suggestion. He was made to stand on a riverbank, tied hand and foot. His daddy, the farmer, was made to watch. Robert was told he had a choice. He could fall off the riverbank by himself, or they could shoot him off. Either way he was going in the water. He was going to drown. Nothing could be done about that part. Robert said, Daddy, help me, and the farmer said, I'm sorry, son, I can't, because I have four more at home, and a farm, and your mother. Robert fell in by himself. Afterward the same county guy came by and said, now you see what happens. He said, voting ain't for you.

Albert said he told Cuthbert all about it, in great detail, in a long letter. About how it didn't even make the local paper. How the county police wrote it up as a disobedient child warned not to swim. Cuthbert wrote back from Paris, depressed but resigned. And impatient. They had fought in the war. How much longer? After that Albert stopped being surprised his brother didn't come home.

---

I drove two hundred miles back the way I had come and took a nap in the passenger seat when I got tired, and then I carried on again. I wanted to get to work. But when I did, I couldn't. I felt ethically the story belonged to the French magazine. But it was a story I didn't want them to have. Or any other nation. I wasn't sure exactly why. Not washing dirty laundry in public, I guessed. United we stand, divided we fall. Clichés were clichés for a reason. I felt like a bad journalist.

Then I realized Cuthbert Jackson had made the same choice. All through the political years. He was Socrates. He could have told a devastating tale. He could have leveraged his exile sky high. But he didn't. He never said a word about Robert. I wondered if he knew exactly why. I wanted to ask him. For a minute I wondered if the magazine would fly me to Paris.

In the end, I stayed home and wrote it up purely as a sidebar. I put, in effect, by the way, Monsieur Jackson has a brother, and this is where he's living, and this is what he's doing. I got paid enough to buy dinner for my friends. We talked about Cuthbert's silence all night long, but we came to no conclusions.

# SHORTY AND THE BRIEFCASE

S horty Malone's legendary week began on Monday, when he got shot in the leg, just barely, in a sanitation department maintenance facility. His squad went in the front door, and another went in the back door, with a vague plan to outflank a guy they knew was concealed somewhere among the parked garbage trucks. Then someone started shooting, and within a split second everyone was shooting. The official report said ninety police rounds were fired that day. No one was killed, not even the concealed guy. The only casualty was Shorty, from an unlucky ricochet. Later reconstructions showed a fellow officer had fired, and his round had taken a gentle deflection off the sidewall of a tire, and then a violent deflection off the chassis rail of a different truck. After that it was badly misshapen and had spent most of its energy. It hit Shorty on the shin bone no worse than a smack with a ball-peen hammer. It broke the skin and cracked the bone. Shorty was immediately hospitalized.

After that it was awkward. It was hard to work up much enthusiasm. Shorty had been in the detective division about a year, so he wasn't a brave rookie anymore, but he wasn't yet a grizzled veteran hero either. He was a nobody. Plus it was technically blue-on-blue. There was even some doubt about whether the concealed guy actually had a gun at all. Plus a rumor it was the wrong guy anyway. Maybe his brother. So the overall feeling was the whole affair would be better forgotten. Which was tough on Shorty. Normally a shot cop would be treated with maximum reverence. Normally Shorty would have been rolling around like a pig in shit. Half a dozen hopeful lowlifes would have started up collections on the internet. Shorty could have been looking at a decent chunk of change. Maybe even college-fund decent.

But he was ignored. On Tuesday we were all reassigned to new duties. Part of forgetting. Sure, way back in history some mistakes might have been made. But that was then. We've moved on. Now we're making progress. We all started learning the new stuff, and as a result, no one went to visit Shorty in the hospital anymore, except his pal Celia Sandstrom, who was another one-year nobody, except better to look at, unless she was wearing her Kevlar vest. Evidently, she stopped by the hospital frequently, and evidently, she kept old Shorty up to date on what was going on. And what wasn't.

We were assigned to Narcotics, as part of their own forgetting. All kinds of previous strategies had come to nothing. It was time to wall them off. Time to move on. Like we had. So that if someone ever mentioned a prior embarrassment, we could all wrinkle our noses and say, "What, that old thing?" Like your girlfriend, when you tell her she looked good in her sweater yesterday. So their department was starting over, too, the same way ours had, and they swapped us in for their big new redemptive idea, which was to stop following the coke, and start following the money. Which needed manpower. Narcotics was a cash business. Cash was like a river. They wanted to see where it flowed. And how. Some parts they knew. Some parts they didn't understand. They wanted us out there, watching.

Specifically, they wanted us watching a guy delivering a briefcase from Jersey. He made the trip usually two times a week. The assumption was the briefcase was packed with paper money. A wholesale payment, maybe, or a share of the profits. One level of the pyramid scheme kicking up to the next. They said a regular briefcase could hold a million dollars. They said it was a physical transfer because money wasn't electronic until it was in a bank. Which cash wasn't yet. They said there was a clue in the name. They said our job was to evaluate the chances of witnessing a hand-to-hand exchange. Which would be two for the price of one. Plus disruption of a vital link in the chain. It was exciting work. No wonder everyone forgot about Shorty. Except Celia. She must have described the mission, the very same day, because that must have been about when Shorty started thinking.

---

The guy with the briefcase was an older gentleman. A person of substance. Somehow powdered and expensive. A very senior figure. His very presence a mark of deep respect. With a million bucks in his hand. The briefcase was metal. Some fancy brand. He carried it along the sidewalk, plain as day, all the way to an old-style office building door. He carried it inside. Ten minutes later he came out without it. We saw him do it exactly the same way the report said he always did it.

The office building had a narrow lobby with security. The directory showed twenty tenants. All bland names. A lot of import and export. No doubt a well-developed grapevine. All kinds of early warning systems. No point in asking questions. We wrote it up and sent it in. Our new bosses didn't like it. They pushed back.

They said, "We need to know which office suite."

We said, "We can't get past the desk."

"Pose as maintenance."

"They don't do maintenance."

"Then use your badge."

"The bad guys would be down the fire escape before the elevator door even opened for us in the lobby. Probably the security guy controls it with a foot pedal."

"Give him a hundred bucks."

"The bad guys give him five."

"Are you proposing to do any work at all?"

We said, "First day, boss. We're looking for leadership."

Afterward Celia said Shorty figured we were missing something. He didn't know what. He was on his back with his leg up in traction. Not medically necessary, but the union thought it would make for a better photograph in the newspaper. Shorty was fretting about us, Celia said. He was missing us.

"Shorty who?" we said.

———

We came in Wednesday morning and as expected found the business with the fancy briefcase already going a little lukewarm. Expectations were being retrospectively downgraded. It was a solid piece of data, another brick in the wall, as intended, nothing more.

Then, even before the coffee was made, it went right back to the top of the agenda. New evidence came in, from a different direction, and it pointed to the same office building. To a specific tenant. They knew for sure the specific guy was sending money out. Now they wanted to square the circle. They wanted to see the same money going in. They wanted eyeballs inside the specific guy's suite. They wanted eyewitness testimony, about the older gentleman maybe placing the briefcase on a table, and the other guy maybe spinning it around and clicking the latches with his thumbs. If we could get close enough to seize the actual cash, well, that would be the icing on the cake.

Afterward Celia said, "Shorty says obviously that's all impossible."

We said, "We don't need the voice of doom drifting down a hospital corridor to tell us that. Of course it's all impossible."

"So what should we do?"

"Nothing. Maybe they'll move us to Vice. Which wouldn't be the worst thing in the world."

But the mention of Shorty recalled the previous mention, at the end of Tuesday, which no detective liked to hear, that we were missing something. No one said anything out loud, but I know we all surreptitiously and individually checked everything we could, from the beginning to the end, in the original files, from the handwritten notes.

The guy drove from Jersey, just him alone at the wheel, no driver, in a nice but unspectacular car, through the Lincoln Tunnel, and south, to a parking garage in the West Twenties, which was the nearest to the old-style office building. A small man in a black vest and a bow tie parked his car, while he walked out with the briefcase and set out carrying it on his long march down the sidewalk. His journey invariably ended after a block and a half in the office building lobby, where he was nodded past the desk after respectful but not casual inspection. On every occasion he spent ten or so minutes inside, and on every occasion he came back out empty-handed. Those were the facts. That was what we knew.

Celia pretended to have given the matter no thought at all, but later she said, "Shorty is sure there's something wrong."

Which was not what we wanted to hear right then, because the stakes had just been raised even higher. A couple more puzzle pieces had fallen into place. Suddenly the folks upstairs realized they could take out the whole chain at once. It would be the bust of the year. Medals for sure. Votes for the mayor. The whole nine yards. But they needed it immaculate. Every link in the chain had to be rock-solid on the witness stand. Evidence was key.

We argued we couldn't get it. We said instead we should bust the guy on the sidewalk, before he got to the office building, with the money still in the briefcase. Because it was legally justified to assume he was heading for the specific guy in the unknown suite. Where else would he be going? It was as good as eyeballing a transfer. Really the same thing, at an earlier stage. A different snapshot. A previous frame from the same movie.

Nothing was ever more persuasive than having no alternative, so they agreed. We waited in a ready room, for a call from Jersey. The local PD over there was watching the guy's residence. Any occasion he drove out in the direction of the tunnel, they would let us know right away. Traffic was usually bad. We would get plenty of warning. No rush at all.

But the call didn't come. Not on Wednesday. Not on Thursday. It came on Friday. Some apple-cheeked trooper out in the burbs told us the guy was on the move in his nice but unspectacular car, and seemed to be heading for Manhattan. Celia was not in the room with us at that point. She came in a minute later and we told her about the call.

She said, "Shorty says we're thinking all wrong."

Which was not what we wanted to hear right then, because we were trying to get all pumped up, ahead of taking a guy down on the sidewalk. But she insisted. She said Shorty had been lying there, with plenty of time to think. We should listen. We were torn. On the one hand, Celia was in the squad. She might be a nobody, but she was ours. Shorty too. On the other hand, the bust of the year was at stake. Medals and votes. Not a thing to screw up by taking the initiative. No one wanted to be the guy who blew it.

Celia said, "Do we really believe it's legally persuasive, if we take him down on the street with a bag of cash?"

"Kind of," we said. "Somewhat. Maybe. Good enough, probably."

"Would his lawyer be worried?"

"A little bit. Maybe not slitting his wrists."

"But whatever, it's a huge hassle, right?" she said. "It's a million bucks in cash. The IRS would get involved. Maybe the Treasury Department. Why take the risk? Why carry that briefcase so openly?"

We said, "We know the cash is moving from A to B. We know the guy inside is receiving it. How else would he be getting it, except from our guy? No one else goes in and out. And people carry all kinds of things in this city. They carry briefcases full of diamonds, worth much more than this guy."

"Shorty thinks it's a decoy. He thinks the case is always empty. They're teasing us. They want us to take the guy down. They're begging us. That's their plan. They want us to open the case and find nothing inside. Shorty says we'll look like fools. He says we'll never get another warrant again. Judges will just laugh at us. We'll have to leave those guys alone for years. That way they win."

We said, "One guy is paying the other guy money. We know that. That's a real fact. Because it's a chain. A lot of people are depending on us to do our part right. We need the evidence."

"We can get it," she said. "But not on the street. That's not where it is. Shorty says you're right, one guy is paying the other guy money. But not the way we think."

"Then how?"

"In the parking garage. The guy leaves the cash in the trunk. Maybe in a supermarket bag. The parking attendant takes it out and puts it in the other guy's car. Which is always there because that garage is convenient for the office building. The real handover is out of sight and out of mind. Everyone is distracted by the shiny briefcase."

No one spoke.

Celia said, "Shorty says it's a win-win for us. We can check the car real quick, as soon as the guy is out of it, and if after all there's nothing in it, then we can always catch up to the guy in a couple of steps, and take him down anyway, like we're supposed to. Shorty says we have nothing to lose."

The phone rang again. The Port Authority cops, at the Jersey mouth of the tunnel. The guy had just come through the E-ZPass.

We got going. We waited in the parking garage.

Nothing to lose.

———

Shorty was right. The cash was in a yellow plastic grocery bag in the trunk of the guy's car. As evidence, it was as good as anyone else got, and better than most folks. It contributed mightily to the bust of the year. In front of Celia we felt inhibited about claiming all the credit for ourselves, so mostly we told the truth, and as a result the story got out quickly, about a hero cop shot in the leg on Monday, who then lay in his hospital bed and fought through the agony and by Friday had engineered one of his new department's most spectacular successes, all through brainpower alone. He got a medal for his leg, and another for the parking garage, and then he was in the newspaper, which is what ultimately made him a legend. The union was right about the photograph. It helped a lot.

# DYING FOR A CIGARETTE

The producer's notes came in. The screenwriter saw the email on his phone. The subject line said *Notes*. The phone was set to preview the first several words of the message, which were *Thanks again for making time for lunch today.* The screenwriter looked away. He didn't open the email. Didn't read more. Instead he backed up and sat down on the sofa, stiff and upright, straight like a poker, palms cupped on the cushions on either side of his knees.

His wife sat down in his lap. She was an hour back from the beauty parlor, still in her afternoon attire, which was a cream silk blouse tucked into a navy linen skirt, which when standing fell just above the knee, and when sitting, especially in a lap, crept a little higher. She was wearing nothing underneath either item. She wondered if he could tell. Probably not, she thought. Not yet. He was preoccupied. She lit a cigarette and placed it between his lips.

He said, "Thank you."

She said, "Tell me about lunch."

"It was him and three of his execs. I think at least one of them was financial."

"How did it go?"

"Exactly like I was afraid it would."

"Exactly?"

"More or less," he said. "Possibly even worse."

She said, "Did you make the speech?"

"What speech?"

"About dying."

"It's only a line. In the first paragraph. Not really a speech."

"Did you say it?"

He nodded, tightly, still a little defiant.

He said, "I told him for years I had been a good little hack, and I had always done what he wanted, as fast as he needed it, overnight sometimes, even sometimes on the fly while the camera was rolling. I told him I had never let him down, and I had made him millions of dollars. So I told him overall I figured I had earned the right to be left alone on this one. Because finally I had the one great idea a guy might ever get in his life. I told him I would rather die than see it compromised."

"That's the speech I was talking about."

"It's only a word."

"With a lot of preamble."

"It's a strong first paragraph, I agree."

"How did he take it?"

"I don't really know. I went out for a cigarette. He was OK when I got back. He said at first he thought I was nuts for not seeing his point, but now I had gotten him thinking maybe I was right and he was wrong."

"What was his issue?"

"This has always been about the British Army in World War One. Am I right? Hasn't it? Since the very first moment I got the idea. You were the very first person I ever talked to about it."

"Actually I think that must have been a previous wife. Or several ago. The idea was already well established when I came on the scene."

"Was it ever anything but the British Army in World War One?"

"Don't they like that?"

"He said the studio asked if it was an English country house movie."

"What was his answer?"

"He said maybe English country house people, but not in the house. Obviously. In the trenches, in France, or Belgium, or wherever else they had trenches."

"So is it a problem?"

"He said the studio thinks the audience would relate better if it was the Civil War. With actual Americans involved."

"I see."

"I reminded him there was an essential story strand involving an airplane pilot. The infancy of technology. A huge metaphor. It could not be dropped or altered in any way. I reminded him that airplanes weren't invented yet, during the Civil War."

"I think they had hot-air balloons."

"Not the same thing at all. A hot-air balloon is automatically a slow-motion scene. We need speed, and fury, and noise, and anger. We need to feel we're on the cusp of something new and dangerous."

"What did he say to all that?"

"He agreed with me the studio's idea was bullshit. He said he only passed it on because it came from the top. He said he never took it seriously. Not for one minute. He was on my side totally. Not just because of the airplanes. Because of the ideas. They're too modern. This all is fifty years after the Civil War. The characters know things people didn't know fifty years before."

"He's right, you know. The ideas are modern. You got it through, even to him. That's great writing, babe."

"He said the same thing. Not babe. He said it was my best writing ever. He said I could say things in four words other writers would need a paragraph for. He said I could get things through, even to a cynical old moneybags like him, about how the thoughts my characters were having were building the postwar world right in front of our eyes."

"Flattering."

"Very."

"He's right, you know," she said again. "It stands to reason. Obviously the postwar world was built from new ideas, and inevitably they were forged during the war itself. But to see history happen in front of our eyes is fantastic. It's going to be a classic. It's a shoo-in for Best Picture."

"Except that the postwar world he was talking about was post–World War Two. The 1950s, in fact. He thinks the story should be set during the Korean War. With actual Americans. And foxholes, not trenches. He thinks foxholes are better. Necessarily more intimate. An automatic reason to shoot a scene with just one or two actors. No extras. No background hoo-ha. Saves a fortune. He said one or two guys alone in a trench would look weird. As in, who are they? Are they malingerers? Did they pull the lucky straw and get to stay behind on sentry duty? Or what? Either way, he figures we would need to burn lines explaining. At the very least we would need to have them say, no, we're not malingerers. It would be an uphill task to get anyone to like them. But guys in a foxhole don't need explaining. They're taking refuge. Maybe there are two of them. They tumbled in together. Maybe it's a shell hole. Maybe it's a little small, so they're resentful of each other right from the start. They have to figure out how to get along. He said the modernity and the futurism in the ideas made no sense in World War One. It had to be the 1950s. He said we could still keep the airplanes. Jet fighter technology was in its infancy. There were the same kind of stresses. All we would need to do was give the guy a more modern kind of helmet. The actual lines could stay the same. He said some things never change. Some truths are eternal."

"How did you react?"

"I let him know I was very angry, and then I went out for another cigarette."

"How long were you gone?"

"I don't know. Ten minutes? Maybe more. It's a big restaurant. It's a long walk from his table even to the lobby."

"You shouldn't do that. Obviously they talk about you, at the table, while you're gone. Him and his people."

"Actually I think they mostly make calls on their phones. Like multitasking. Probably trashing other writers' dreams. I saw them finishing up when I came back in, every time. They were looking kind of guilty about it."

"You should watch your back."

"It doesn't matter if they talk about me anyway. They can't make me agree. This is my project. I could take it somewhere else."

"Where?"

The screenwriter didn't answer.

His wife snuggled tighter. She pressed her chest against his. No bra. She wondered if he could tell yet. She felt like he should. Certainly she could. Just a thin layer of silk.

She said, "He might be right about the foxholes."

"The point is the whole structure of English society was reproduced in the trenches. The officers had servants and separate quarters. It was a microcosm. We need it as a baseline assumption. Like a framework for the story."

"But a foxhole could reproduce American society just the same. Kind of quick and dirty, kind of temporary. Two recent arrivals, required to somehow get along together. Like a metaphor of its own. Maybe one of them could have been drafted out of Harvard or Princeton or somewhere, and the other is a street kid from Boston or the Bronx. At first they have nothing in common."

"Cliché."

"So is a country house drama with mud. You were a good enough writer to make that work. You could make anything work."

He said, "That's not the worst of it."

"What more?"

"He said the hero can't be a loner. He said there has to be a buddy, from the first scene onward."

"Really?"

"He said he realized all along in the back of his mind he had been seeing it as a buddy movie set in Korea. He said my draft was the right heart in the wrong body. He said it wasn't a story about one Englishman. It was a story about two Americans. He said sometimes writers don't truly understand what they've written."

"What did you say?"

"Nothing. I was speechless. I went out for another cigarette."

"How long this time?"

"The same. Ten minutes. Maybe more. But don't worry. What was there to talk about? Suddenly I realized I had gotten it ass-backward. I thought I was owed one particular thing, because I had been a good worker. They thought I was owed a different thing. Which was not to laugh in my face and turn the picture down flat. They were looking for a polite exit strategy. Ideally they wanted me to withdraw the proposal. That would save everyone's face. Artistic differences. So they were nibbling it to death. Trying to make me break."

"Did you?"

"Turned out I was wrong. They were serious. I got back in and started to say something about how we had all agreed at the get-go that the artistic vision would not be compromised, ever, in any way, and now here we were with two best buds in Korea. But he cut me off early and said, sure, don't worry, he understood. He said I had to remember every single idea in the history of the motion picture industry had gotten a little scuffed up when it came out of the writer's head and collided with reality. Even the famous screenplays that get studied in film school. The lady who brought the coffee added some of the lines. It was about what worked on the day."

"What did you say?"

"Nothing."

"You didn't go out again, did you?"

"I wanted to. I wanted to register some kind of protest. But I didn't need to go out. Not even me. So I stayed at the table. He took it as an invitation to keep on talking. He said I could reclaim the movie by writing a great death scene."

"Reclaim it?"

"He said I could own it again."

"Whose death?"

"The buddy's. Obviously the hero has to be alone for the final stage of his journey. So the buddy has to go, page ninety or thereabouts. He said he was sure I would knock it out of the park. Not just the final flutter. But the reasons for it. What was driving that guy to his doom?"

"What did you say?"

"Nothing. My head was spinning. First a completely unnecessary secondary character was being forced into my movie, thereby making it actually no longer my movie, but then I'm being told it can be my movie again if I yank the intruder out again. Seemed staggeringly Freudian to me. He had such faith I could do it. He said it will be my finest work. Which would be ironic. Maybe the Writers Guild would give me a special award. Best Death of a Producer-Imposed Trope."

"What happened next?"

"I left. I skipped dessert. I came home."

"I'm glad," she said.

She snuggled closer.

She said, "But I'm sorry the world will never see that scene. He was right about that, at least. You would have knocked it out of the park. Some kind of noble sacrifice. One for the ages."

"No," he said. "Not noble. I think I would make it small. The big things have already been done. The friendship has been forged. I suppose the final scene has to be in a foxhole. The two of them. They've gotten that far by being strong. Now the buddy is about to exit the picture by being weak. That's the dynamic. I think that's the way battle movies have got to work. Personality is revealed by the big things first and the little things last."

"Weak how?"

"This is the 1950s, don't forget. Even the studio doesn't want to drag it into the present day. So people smoked. Including the buddy. Now he's in the foxhole and he's out of cigarettes. He's getting antsy. People smoking means it's already an R-rated movie anyway, so twenty yards away we can have the mangled corpse of one of their squad mates, who the buddy knows is an occasional smoker, which almost certainly means he's got a nearly full pack in his pocket."

"Twenty yards beyond the rim of the foxhole?"

"And there's an enemy sniper in the area."

"Does he stay, or does he go?"

"He goes," the screenwriter said. "Twenty yards there, twenty yards back. The sniper gets him. It's both tiny and monumental. He wanted a cigarette. That was all. A small human weakness. But it was also a determination to live the way he wanted to, or not live at all. Which then explains and informs his earlier actions. We know him fully only at the moment of his death."

His wife said, "That's lovely."

She snuggled even tighter and scooched her butt even closer.

She said, "So really it's a fairly small decision. Isn't it? It's English accents in 1916, or American accents in 1952. Does it matter?"

He didn't answer. He had noticed.

———

Two years and seven months later the movie came out. It was not about the British Army in World War One. It was compromised in every possible way. The screenwriter did not throw himself under a train. Instead he moved house, higher up the canyon. Then eight months later the buddy won the Oscar. Best Actor in a Supporting Role. The guy's speech was all about how fabulous the writing was. Then an hour later the screenwriter won an Oscar of his own. Best Original Screenplay. His speech thanked his wife and his producer, the rocks in his life. Coming off the stage he pumped the statuette like a heavy dumbbell and figured some compromises were easy to live with. They got easier and easier through the after-parties and the interviews and the calls from his agent, which for the first time in his life gave him a choice of what to do and when and how much for. The years passed and he became a name, then a senior figure, then a guru. He and his wife stayed married. They lived a great life. He was honestly happy.

He never twigged exactly how his ancient compromises had been engineered. What had killed his artistic vision had been his cigarette breaks. They were ten-minute voids, ripe for exploitation. It was the producer's idea. He had done it before with difficult writers. As soon as the guy stalked out, he would call the guy's wife, to report the latest impasse, to get advice on what to say in the short term, to talk him down off the ledge, and then to build an agenda for the wife to discuss with the guy that night, strictly in his own best interests, of course, for his own good, because there was a lot of money and prestige on the line here, and in the producer's experience a little grumpiness would be quickly forgotten when there was a gold statuette to polish. In this case the wife thought, *He's right, you know*, and he was.

# THE SNAKE EATER
# BY THE NUMBERS

Numbers. Percentages, rates, averages, means, medians. Crime rate, clearance rate, clearance percentage, increase, decrease, throughput, input, output, productivity. At the end of the twentieth century, police work was about nothing but numbers.

Detective Sergeant Ken Cameron loved numbers.

I know this, because Cameron was my training officer the year he died. He told me that numbers were our salvation. They made being a copper as easy as being a financier or a salesman or a factory manager. We don't need to work the cases, he said. We need to work the *numbers*. If we make our numbers, we get good performance reviews. If we get good reviews, we get commendations. If we get commendations, we get promotions. And promotions mean pay and pensions. You could be comfortable your whole life, he said, because of numbers. Truly comfortable. Doubly comfortable, he said, because you're not tearing your hair out over vague bullshit subjective notions like safe streets and quality of life. You're dealing with numbers, and numbers never lie.

We worked in North London. Or at least he did, and I was assigned there for my probationary period. I would be moving on, but he had been there three years and would be staying. And North London was a great place for numbers. It was a big manor with a lot of crime and a population that was permanently hypersensitive to being treated less well than populations in other parts of London. The local councillors were always in an uproar. They compared their schools to other schools, their transport spurs to other transport spurs. Everything was about perceived disadvantage. If an escalator was out at the West Finchley tube station for three days, then they better not hear that an escalator had been fixed in two days down at Tooting Bec. That kind of thing was the birth of the numbers, Cameron told me. Because stupid, dull administrators learned to counter the paranoid arguments with numbers. No, they would say, the Northern Line is actually sixty-three percent on time up here, and only sixty-one percent on time down there.

So, they would say, shut up.

It wasn't long before police work fell in with the trend. It was inevitable. Everything started being measured. It was an obvious defensive tactic on the part of our bosses. Average response time following a 999 call? Eleven minutes in Tottenham, Madam

Councillor, versus twelve minutes in Kentish Town. Said proudly, with a blank-but-smug expression on our bosses' meaty faces. Of course, they were lying. The Kentish Town bosses were lying too. It was a race toward absurdity. I once joked to Cameron that pretty soon we would start to see negative response times. Like, Yes, Madam Councillor, that 999 call was answered eleven minutes before it was made. But Cameron just stared at me. He thought I had lost it. He was far too serious on the subject to countenance such a blatant mistake, even in jest.

But certainly he admitted that numbers could be massaged.

He collected massage examples like a connoisseur. He observed some of them from afar. The 999 stuff, for instance. He knew how the books were cooked. Switchboard operators were required to be a little inexact with their timekeeping. When it was noon out there in the real world, it was four minutes past noon inside the emergency switchboard. When a sector car was dispatched to an address, it would radio its arrival when it was still three streets away. Thus, a slow twenty-minute response time went into the books as a decent twelve minutes. Everybody won.

His approach to his own numbers was more sophisticated.

His major intellectual preoccupation was parsing the inconvenient balance between his productivity and his clearance rate. For any copper, the obvious way to enhance his clearance rate was to accept no cases at all, except the solid gold slam dunks that had guaranteed collars at the end of them. He explained it like a Zen master: Suppose you have only one case a year. Suppose you solve it. What's your clearance rate? One hundred percent! I knew that, of course, because I was comfortable with simple arithmetic. But just for fun I said, OK, but suppose you don't solve it? Then your clearance rate is zero! But he didn't get all wound up like I thought he would. Instead, he beamed at me, like I was making progress. Like I already knew the dance steps. Exactly, he said. You avoid the cases you know you can't solve, and you jump all over the cases you know you can solve.

I should have spotted it right then. The cases you know you can solve. But I didn't spot it. I was still inside the box. And he didn't give me much time to think, because he rushed straight on to the main problem, which was productivity. Certainly major points could be scored for a seventy-five percent clearance rate. That was obvious. But if you achieved that mark by clearing three cases out of four, you lost major points for a lack of productivity. That was obvious, too. Four cases a year was absurdly low. Forty cases a year was low. In North London at that time, each detective was looking at hundreds of cases a year. That was Ken Cameron's big problem. The balance between productivity and clearance rate. Good productivity meant a bad clearance rate. A good clearance rate meant bad productivity. He said to me, See? Like the weight of the world was on his shoulders. Although that was a misinterpretation on my part. He was really saying: So I'm not such a bad guy, doing what I'm doing. I should have seen it. But I didn't.

Then, still in his Zen master mode, he told me a joke. Two guys are in the woods. They see a bear coming. "Run!" says the first guy. "That's ridiculous," the second guy says. "You can't run faster than a bear." "I don't need to run faster than the bear," the first guy answers. "I only need to run faster than you." I had heard the joke before, many times. I suppose I paused a moment to remember who had told it to me last. So I didn't react the way Cameron wanted me to. I saw him thinking fast-track–training college wanker. Then he regrouped and explained his point. He wasn't looking for extremely high numbers in and of themselves. He was just looking to beat the guy in second place. That's all. By a point or two, which was all that was necessary. Which he could do while maintaining an entirely plausible balance between his clearance rate and his productivity.

Which he could do. I should have asked, how exactly? He was probably waiting for me to ask. But I didn't.

I found out how the day I met a prostitute called Kelly Key and a madman called Mason Mason. I met them separately. Kelly Key first. It was one of those perceived disadvantage things. Truth was, North London had a lot of prostitution, but not nearly as much as the West End, for instance. It tended to be of a different nature, though. It was definitely more in-your-face. You saw the hookers. Up west, they were all inside, waiting by the phone. So I was never really sure exactly what the locals were up in arms about. That their hookers were cheaper? That they wanted prettier girls? Or what? But whatever, there was always some street-clearing initiative going on, usually in the northern reaches of Islington and all over Haringey. Working girls would be dragged in. They would sit in police stations, looking completely at home and completely out of place all at the same time.

One morning we got back from the canteen and found Kelly Key waiting. Ken Cameron evidently took a snap decision and decided to use her to teach me all kinds of essential things. He took me aside and started to explain. First, we were not going to write anything down. Writing something down would put her in the system, which would aid our productivity, but which would damage our clearance rate, because solicitation cases were very hard to make. But, the longer we concealed our indifference, the more worried old Kelly would get, which would result in some excellent freebies after we finally let her go. A cop who pays for sex, Cameron told me, is a very bad cop indeed.

Bad cop. I suppose, in a relative way.

So I watched while Cameron harassed Kelly Key. It was late morning, but she was already dressed in her hooker outfit. I could see a lot of leg and a lot of cleavage. She wasn't dumb enough to offer anything off her own bat, but she was heavily into doing the Sharon Stone thing from *Basic Instinct*. She was crossing and uncrossing her legs so fast I could almost feel the disturbance in the air. Cameron was enjoying the interview. And the actual view, I suppose. I could see that. He was totally at his ease. He had the upper hand, so definitively it was just an absolute fact. He was a big man, fleshy and solid in that classic policeman way. He was probably forty-something, although it's hard to be precise with guys who have that sort of tight pink flesh on their faces. But he had his size, and his badge, and his years in, and together they made him invulnerable. Or together they had, so far.

Then Mason Mason was brought in. We still had an hour of fun to go with Kelly, but we heard a disturbance at the front desk. Mason Mason had been arrested for urinating in public. At that time we called the uniformed coppers woollies, because of their wool uniforms, and on the face of it the woollies could handle public urination on their own, even if they wanted to

push the charge upward toward gross indecency. But Mason
Mason had been searched and found with a little more folding
money in his pocket than street people usually carry. He had
£90 on him, in new tenners. So the woollies brought him to us,
in case we might want to try a theft charge, or mugging, or even
robbery with violence, because maybe he had pushed someone
around to get the cash. It might be a slam dunk. The woollies
weren't dumb. They knew how we balanced clearance rate with
productivity, and they were self-interested too, because although
individual detectives competed among themselves, there was
also an overall station number, which helped everybody. There
was a number for everything.

So at that point Cameron put Kelly Key on the back burner
and Mason Mason on the front. He took me aside to explain a
few things. First, Mason Mason was the guy's actual name. It was
on his birth certificate. It was widely believed that his father had
been drunk or confused or both at the Registry Office and had
written Mason in both boxes, first name and surname. Second,
Mason wasn't pissing in public because he was a helpless drunk or
derelict. In fact, he rarely drank. In fact, he was pretty harmless.
The thing was, although Mason had been born in Tottenham—in
a house very near the Spurs ground—he believed he was American
and believed he had served in the United States Marine Corps,
as part of Force Recon, who called themselves the Snake Eaters.
This, Cameron said, was both a delusion and an unshakable conviction. North London was full of dedicated Elvis impersonators,
and country and western singers, and Civil War reenactors, and
Omaha Beach buffs, and vintage Cadillac drivers, so Mason's view

of himself wasn't totally extraordinary. But it led to awkwardness. He believed that the North London streets were in fact part of the ruined cityscape of Beirut, and that to step into the rubble and take a leak against the shattered remains of a building was all part of a marine's hard life. And he was always collecting insignias and badges and tattoos. He had snake tattoos all over his body, including one on his chest, along with the words Don't Tread On Me.

After absorbing all this information I glanced back at Mason and noticed that he was wearing a single snake earring, in his left ear. It was a fat little thing, all in heavy gold, quite handsome, quite tightly curled. It had a tiny gold loop at the top, with a non-matching silver hook through it that went up and through his pierced lobe.

Cameron noticed it, too.

"That's new," he said. "The Snake Eater's got himself another bauble."

Then his eyes went blank for a second, like a TV screen changing channels.

I should have seen it coming.

He sent Kelly Key away to sit by herself and started in on Mason. First he embarrassed him by asking routine questions, starting with a request that he should state his name.

"Sir, the marine's name is Mason, sir," the guy said, just like a marine.

"Is that your first or last name?"

"Sir, both, sir," the guy said.

"Date of birth?"

Mason reeled off day, month, year. It put him pretty close to what I guessed was Cameron's age. He was about Cameron's size, too, which was unusual for a bum. Mostly they waste away. But Mason Mason was tall and heavily built. He had hands the size of Tesco chickens and a neck that was wider than his head. The earring looked out of place, all things considered, except maybe in some kind of a pirate context. But I could see why the woollies thought that robbery with violence might fly. Most people would hand over their wad to Mason Mason, rather than stand and fight.

"Place of birth?" Cameron asked.

"Sir, Muncie, Indiana, sir," Mason said.

The way he spoke told me he was clearly from London, but his faux-American accent was pretty impressive. Clearly he watched a lot of TV and spent a lot of time in the local multiplexes. He had worked hard to become a marine. His eyes were good, too. Flat, wary, expressionless. Just like a real jarhead's. I guessed he had seen *Full Metal Jacket* more than once.

"Muncie, Indiana," Cameron repeated. "Not Tottenham? Not North London?"

"Sir, no sir," Mason barked. Cameron laughed at him, but Mason kept his face blank, just like a guy who had survived boot camp.

"Military service?" Cameron asked.

"Sir, eleven years in God's own Marine Corps, sir."

"Semper fi?"

"Sir, roger that, sir."

"Where did you get the money, Mason?"

It struck me that when a guy has the same name first and last, it's impossible to come across too heavy. For instance, suppose I said Hey, Ken, to Cameron? I would sound friendly. If I said Hey, Cameron, I would sound accusatory. But it was all the same to Mason Mason.

"I won the money," he said. Now he sounded like a sullen Londoner.

"On a horse?"

"On a dog. At Haringey."

"When?"

"Last night."

"How much?"

"Ninety quid."

"Marines go dog racing?"

"Sir, recon marines blend in with the local population." Now he was a jarhead again.

"What about the earring?" Cameron asked. "It's new."

Mason touched it as he spoke.

"Sir, it was a gift from a grateful civilian."

"What kind of civilian?"

"A woman in Kosovo, sir."

"What did she have to be grateful about?"

"Sir, she was about to be a victim of ethnic cleansing."

"At whose hands?"

"The Serbs, sir."

"Wasn't it the Bosnians?"

"Whoever, sir. I didn't ask questions."

"What happened?" Cameron asked.

"There was social discrimination involved," Mason said. "People considered rich were singled out for special torment. A family was considered rich if the wife owned jewelry. Typically the jewelry would be assembled and the husband would be forced to eat it. Then the wife would be asked if she wanted it back. Typically she would be confused and unsure of the expected answer. Some would say yes, whereupon the aggressors would slit the husband's stomach open and force the wife to retrieve the items herself."

"And you prevented this from happening?"

"Me and my men, sir. We mounted a standard fire-and-maneuver encirclement of a simple dwelling and took down the aggressors. It was a modest household, sir. The woman owned just a single pair of earrings."

"And she gave them to you."

"Just one, sir. She kept the other one."

"She gave you an earring?"

"In gratitude, sir. Her husband's life was saved."

"When was this?"

"Sir, our operational log records the engagement at 0400 last Thursday."

Cameron nodded. He left Mason Mason at the desk and pulled me away into the corner. We competed for a minute or two with all the one-sandwich-short-of-a-picnic metaphors we knew. One brick shy of a load, not the sharpest knife in the drawer, that kind of thing. I felt bad about it later. I should have seen what was coming.

But Cameron was already into another long and complicated calculation. It was almost metaphysical in its complexity. If we logged another case today, our productivity number would rise.

Obviously. If we broke it, our clearance rate would rise. Obviously. Question was, would our clearance rate rise faster than our productivity number? Basically, was it worth it? The equation seemed to me to require some arcane calculus, which was beyond me, and I was a fast-track–training college wanker. But Cameron seemed to have a handy rule of thumb. He seemed to suggest that it's always worth logging a case if you know you're going to break it. At the time I suspected that was a non-mathematical superstition, but I couldn't prove it. Still can't, actually, without going to night school. But back then I didn't argue the arithmetic. I argued the facts instead.

"Do we even have a case?" I asked.

"Let's find out," he said.

I imagined he would send me out for an *Evening Standard*, so we could check the greyhound results from Haringey. Or he would send me to wade through incident reports, looking for a stolen snake earring from last Thursday night. But he did neither thing. He walked me back to Kelly Key instead.

"You work hard for your money, right?" he said to her.

I could see that Kelly didn't know where that question was going. Was she being sympathized with, or propositioned? She didn't know. She was in the dark. But like all good whores everywhere, she came up with a neutral answer.

"It can be fun," she said. "With some men."

She didn't add, Men like you. That would have been too blatant. Cameron might have been setting a trap. But the way she smiled and touched his forearm with her fingertips left the words, It can be fun with men like you hanging right there in the air. Certainly

Cameron heard them, loud and clear. But he just shook his head, impatiently.

"I'm not asking for a date," he said.

"Oh," she said.

"I'm just saying, you work hard for your money."

She nodded. The smile disappeared and I saw reality flood her face. She worked very hard for her money. That message was unmistakable.

"Doing all kinds of distasteful things," Cameron said.

"Sometimes," she said.

"How much do you charge?"

"Two hundred for the hour."

"Liar," Cameron said. "The twenty-two-year-olds up west charge two hundred for the hour."

Kelly nodded.

"Fifty for a quickie," she said.

"How about thirty?"

"I could do that."

"How would you feel if a punter ripped you off?"

"Like he didn't pay?"

"Like he stole ninety quid from you. That's like not paying four times. You end up doing him for nothing, and you end up doing the previous three guys for nothing too, because now that money's gone."

"I wouldn't like it," she said.

"Suppose he stole your earring, as well?"

"My what?"

"Your earring."

"Who?"

Cameron looked across the room at Mason. Kelly Key followed his gaze.

"Him?" she said. "I wouldn't do him. He's mad."

"Suppose you did."

"I wouldn't."

"We're playing let's-pretend here," Cameron said. "Suppose you did him, and he stole your money and your earring."

"That's not even a real earring."

"Isn't it?"

Kelly shook her head. "It's a charm from a charm bracelet. You guys are hopeless. Couldn't you see that? It's supposed to be fastened onto a bracelet. Through that little hoop at the top? You can see the wire doesn't match."

We all stared at Mason Mason's ear. Then I looked at Cameron. I saw his eyes do the blank thing again. The channel-changing thing.

"I could arrest you, Kelly Key," he said.

"But?"

"But I won't, if you play ball."

"Play ball how?"

"Swear out a statement that Mason Mason stole ninety quid and a charm bracelet from you."

"But he didn't."

"What part of let's-pretend don't you understand?"

Kelly Key said nothing.

"You could leave out your professional background," Cameron said. "If you want to. Just say he broke into your house. While you were in bed asleep. The homeowner being in bed asleep always goes down well."

Kelly Key took her gaze off Mason. Turned back to Cameron.

"Would I get my stuff back afterward?" she asked.

"What stuff?"

"The ninety quid and the bracelet. If I'm saying he stole them from me, then they were mine to begin with, weren't they? So I should get them back."

"Jesus Christ," Cameron said.

"It's only fair."

"The bracelet is imaginary. How the hell can you get it back?"

"It can't be imaginary. There's got to be evidence."

Cameron's eyes went blank again. The channel changed. He told Kelly to stay where she was and pulled me back across the room, to the corner.

"We can't just manufacture a case," I said.

He looked at me, exasperated. Like the idiot child.

"We're not manufacturing a case," he said. "We're manufacturing a number. There's a big difference."

"How is there? Mason will still go to jail. That's not a number."

"Mason will be better off," he said. "I'm not totally heartless. Ninety quid and a bracelet from a whore, he'll get three months, tops. They'll give him psychiatric treatment. He doesn't get any on the outside. They'll put him back on his meds. He'll come out a new man. It's like putting him in a clinic. A rest home. At public expense. It's doing him a favor."

I said nothing.

"Everyone's a winner," he said.

227

I said nothing.

"Don't rock the boat, kid," he said.

I didn't rock the boat. I should have, but I didn't.

He led me back to where Mason Mason was sitting. He told Mason to hand over his new earring. Mason unhooked it from his earlobe without a word and gave it to Cameron. Cameron gave it to me. The little snake was surprisingly heavy in the palm of my hand, and warm.

Then Cameron led me downstairs to the evidence lockup. Public whining had created a lot of things, he said, as far as police work went. It had created the numbers, and the numbers had been used to get budgets, and the budgets were huge. No politician could resist padding police budgets. Not local, not national. So most of the time we were flush with money. The problem was, how to spend it? They could have put more woollies on the street, or they could have doubled the number of CID thief-takers, but bureaucrats like monuments, so mostly they spent it on building new police stations. North London was full of them. There were big concrete bunkers all over the place. Manors had been split and amalgamated and HQs had been shifted around. The result was that evidence lockups all over North London were full of old stuff that had been dragged in from elsewhere. Stuff that was historic. Stuff that nobody tracked anymore.

Cameron sent the desk sergeant out for lunch and started looking for the pre-film record books. He told me that extremely recent stuff was logged on the computers, and slightly older stuff was recorded on microfilm, and the stuff from twenty or thirty years ago was still in the original handwritten logbooks. That was the stuff to steal, he said, because you could just tear out the relevant page. No way to take a page off a microfilm, without taking a hundred other pages with it. And he had heard that deleting stuff from computer files left telltale traces, even when it shouldn't.

So we split up the pile of dusty old logbooks and started trawling through them, looking for charm bracelets lost or recovered years ago in the past. Cameron told me we were certain to find one. He claimed there was at least one of everything in a big police evidence lockup like this one. Artificial limbs, oil paintings, guns, clocks, heroin, watches, umbrellas, shoes, wedding rings, anything you needed. And he was right. The books I looked at told me there was a Santa's grotto behind the door behind the desk.

It was me who found the bracelet. It was right there in the third book I went through. I should have kept quiet and just turned the page. But I was new and I was keen, and I suppose to some extent I was under Cameron's spell. And I didn't want to rock the boat. I had a career ahead of me, and I knew what would help it and what would hurt it. So I didn't turn the page. Instead, I called out.

"Got one," I said.

Cameron closed his own book and came over and took a look at mine. The listing read Charm Bracelet, female, one, gold, some charms attached. The details related to some ancient long-forgotten case from the 1970s.

"Excellent," Cameron said.

The lockup itself was what I supposed the back room of an Argos looked like. There was all kinds of stuff in boxes, stacked all over shelves that were ten feet high. There was a comprehensive numbering system with everything stacked in order, but it all got a little haphazard with the really old stuff. It took us a minute or two to find the right section. Then Cameron slid a small cardboard box off a shelf and opened it.

"Bingo," he said.

It wasn't a jeweler's box. It was just something from an old office supplier. There was no cotton wool inside. Just the charm bracelet itself. It was a handsome thing, quite heavy, very gold. There were charms on it. I saw a key, and a cross, and a little tiger. Plus some other small items I couldn't identify.

"Put the snake on it," Cameron said. "It's got to look right."

There were closed loops on the circumference of the bracelet that matched the closed loop on the top of Mason's snake. I found an empty one. But having two closed loops didn't help me.

"I need gold wire," I said.

"Back to the books," Cameron said.

We put his one of everything claim to the test. And sure enough, we came up with Gold Wire, jeweler's, one coil. Lost property, from 1969. Cameron cut a half-inch length with his pocket knife.

"I need pliers," I said.

"Use your fingernails," he said.

It was difficult work, but I got it secure enough. Then the whole thing disappeared into Cameron's pocket.

"Go tear out the page," he said.

I shouldn't have, but I did.

I got a major conscience attack four days later. Mason Mason had been arrested. He pled not guilty in front of the magistrates, and they remanded him for trial and set bail at five thousand pounds. I think Cameron had colluded with the prosecution service to set the figure high enough to keep Mason off the street, because he was a little worried about him. Mason was a big guy, and he had been very angry about the fit-up. Very angry. He said he knew the filth had to make their numbers. He was OK with that. But he said nobody should accuse a marine of dishonor. Not ever. So he stewed for a couple of days. And then he surprised everyone by making bail. He came up with the money and walked. Everyone speculated but nobody knew where the cash came from. Cameron was nervous for a day, but he got over it. Cameron was a big guy too, and a copper.

Then the next day I saw Cameron with the bracelet. It was late in the afternoon. He had it out on his desk. He slipped it into his pocket when he noticed me.

"That should be back in the lockup," I said. "With a new case number. Or it should be on Kelly Key's wrist."

"I gave her the ninety quid," he said. "I decided I'm keeping the bracelet."

"Why?"

"Because I like it."

"No, why?" I said.

"Because there's a pawn shop I know in Muswell Hill."

"You're going to sell it?"

He said nothing.

"I thought this was about the numbers," I said.

"There's more than one kind of numbers," he said. "There's pounds in my pocket. That's a number too."

"When are you going to sell it?"

"Now."

"Before the trial? Don't we need to produce it for evidence?"

"You're not thinking, kid. The bracelet's gone. He fenced it already. How do you think he came up with the bail money? Juries like nice little consistencies like that."

Then he left me alone at my desk. That's when the conscience attack kicked in. I started thinking about Mason Mason. I wanted to make sure he wasn't going to suffer for our numbers. If he was going to get medical treatment in jail, well, fine. I could live with that. It was wrong, but maybe it was right, too. But how could we guarantee it? I supposed it would depend on his record. If there was previous psychiatric treatment, maybe it would be continued as a matter of routine. But what if there wasn't? What if there had been a previous determination that he was just a sane-but-bad guy? Right then and there I decided I would go along to get along only if Mason was going to make out OK. If he wasn't, then I would torpedo the whole thing. Including my own career. That was my pact with the devil. That's the only thing I can offer in my defense.

I fired up my computer.

His name being the same first and last eliminated any confusion about who I was looking for. There was only one Mason Mason in London. I worked backward through his history. At first, it was very encouraging. He had had psychiatric treatment. He had been brought in many times for various offenses, all of them related to his conviction that he was a recon marine and London was a battlefield. He built bivouacs in parks. He went to the toilet in public. Occasionally he assaulted passersby because he thought they were Shi'ite guerrillas or Serbian militia. But generally the police had treated him well. They were usually kind and understanding. They got the mental health professionals involved as often as possible. He received treatment. Reading the transcripts in reverse date order made it seem like they were treating him better and better. Which meant in reality they were tiring of him somewhat. They were actually getting shorter and shorter with him. But they understood. He was nuts. He wasn't a criminal. So, OK.

Then I noticed something.

There was nothing recorded more than three years old. No, that was wrong. I scrolled way back and found there was in fact some very old stuff. Stuff from fourteen years previously. He had been in his late twenties then and in regular trouble for public disorder. Scuffles, fights, wild drunkenness, bodily harm. Some heavy-duty stuff, but normal stuff. Not mental stuff.

I heard Cameron's voice in my head: He rarely drinks. He's pretty harmless.

I thought: Two Mason Masons. The old one, and the new one.

With an eleven-year gap between.

I heard Mason's own voice in my head, with its impressive American twang: Sir, eleven years in God's own Marine Corps, sir.

I sat still for a minute.

Then I picked up the phone and called the American Embassy, down in Grosvenor Square. I couldn't think of anything else to do. I identified myself as a police officer. They put me through to a military attaché.

"Is it possible for a foreign citizen to serve in your Marine Corps?" I asked.

"You thinking of volunteering?" the guy answered. "Bored with being a cop?" His voice was a little like Mason's. I wondered whether he had been born in Muncie, Indiana.

"Is it possible?" I asked again.

"Sure it is," he said. "At any one time we've got a pretty healthy percentage of foreign nationals in uniform. It's a job, after all, and it gets them citizenship in three years instead of five."

"Can you check records from there?"

"Is it urgent?"

I thought of Cameron on his way to Muswell Hill. Being shadowed by a recon marine with a grudge.

"It's very urgent," I said.

"Who are we looking for?"

"A guy called Mason."

"First name?"

"Mason."

"No, first name."

"Mason," I said. "Both his names are Mason."

"Hold the line," he said.

I spent the time working out Cameron's likely route. He would probably walk. Too short a journey to drive, too awkward on the tube. So he would walk. He would walk through Alexandra Park.

"Hello?" the guy at the embassy said.

"Yes?"

"Mason Mason served eleven years in the Marines. Originally a UK citizen. Made the rank of First Sergeant. He was selected for

Force Recon and served all over. Beirut, Panama, the Gulf, Kosovo. Received multiple decorations and an honorable discharge just over three years ago. He was a damn fine jarhead. But there's a file note here saying he was just in some kind of trouble. One of the Overseas Veterans' associations just had to bail him out from something."

"Why did he leave the Marines?"

"He failed a psychiatric evaluation."

"You get an honorable discharge for that?"

"We kick them out," the guy said. "We don't kick them in the teeth."

---

I sat there for a moment, undecided. Should I dispatch sector cars? They would be no good in the park. Should I send the woollies on foot? Was I overreacting?

I went on my own, running all the way.

It was late in the year and late in the day and it was already going dark. I crossed the railway as a train rumbled under the bridge I was on. I watched the road ahead, and the hedges on each side. I didn't see Cameron. I didn't see Mason.

Alexandra Park's iron gates were already closed and locked. This facility closes at dusk, said the sign. I climbed over the gates and ran onward. The smell of night mist was already in the air. I could hear distant traffic all the way from the North Circular. I could hear starlings roosting somewhere to the south. In Hornsey, maybe. I followed the main path and found nothing. I saw the dark bulk of Alexandra Palace ahead and stood still. Go on or turn back?

The streets of Muswell Hill, or the park? Surely the park was the danger zone. The park was where a recon marine would do his work. I turned back.

I found Cameron a yard off a side path.

He was half hidden under some low shrubbery. He was on his back. His coat was missing. His jacket was missing. His shirt had been torn off. He was naked from the waist up. He had been ripped open from the sternum to the navel with a sharp blade. Then someone had plunged his hands inside the wound and lifted his stomach out whole and rested it on his chest. Just pulled it out, the whole organ. It was right there on his chest, pale and purple and veined. Like a soft balloon. It had been squeezed and pressed and palpated and arranged until the faint gold gleam of the charm bracelet showed through the thin translucent lining. I saw it quite clearly, in the fading evening light.

I think I was supposed to play the part of the Kosovo wife. I was Cameron's coconspirator, and I was supposed to recover the jewelry. Or Kelly Key was. But neither of us did. Mason's tableau came to nothing. I didn't try, and Kelly Key never even saw the body.

———

I didn't report it. I just got out of the park that night and left him there for someone else to find the next morning. And someone else did, of course. It was a big sensation. There was a big funeral. Everyone went. Then there was a big investigation, obviously. I contributed nothing, but even so Mason Mason became the prime suspect. But he disappeared and was never seen again. He's still out there somewhere, a mad recon marine blending in with the local population, wherever he is.

And me? I completed my probationary year and now I'm a Detective Constable down in Tower Hamlets. I've been there a couple of years. My numbers are pretty good. Not quite as good as Ken Cameron's were, but then, I try to live and learn.